1969
Road Trip Isfahan
and
Other Rites of Passage

Piers Rowlandson

Road trip Isfahan 1969

Copyright © 2018 Piers Rowlandson

All rights reserved.

ISBN: 9781724158086

For obvious reasons, it is important to state that all the people and incidents in this novel are imaginary.

Road trip Isfahan 1969

Dedication
To my children
"Tread softly because you tread on my dreams."
W B Yeats

Road trip Isfahan 1969

Contents

1. Rick arrives in Oxford
2. Oxford to the Dordogne
3. Dordogne to Yugoslavia
4. Yugoslavia to Thessaloniki
5. Thessaloniki to Istanbul
6. Istanbul to Trabzon
7. The Black Sea
8. Trabzon to Mianduab
9. Mianduab to Baba Jan
10. Baba Jan
11. Annabel Gets a Fever
12. Baba Jan to Isfahan
13. Tehran to the Caspian Sea
14. Tehran to Istanbul
15. Istanbul to Oxford
16. A Party in Oxford
17. Back in London
18. Summertime in the USA
19. The Wedding
20. Annabel's Illness
21. Rick Leaves London

Road trip Isfahan 1969

Chapter One
Rick arrives in Oxford

"Excuse me," and then louder, "excuse me!"

The girl looked round. She was a short girl with dark hair tied back in a ponytail. Rick leaned out of the Land Rover and smiled.

"Sorry, I didn't mean to startle you, but do you know the way to Rawlinson Avenue, it is just off the Banbury Road but I can't seem to find it."

"You've just passed it. The name is hidden in the hedge, it's just back there."

She grinned, turned and walked away, swinging her bag.

"Thanks so much!" he called after the retreating figure, hoping she would turn round. She didn't.

Rick drove into the half circle of drive in front of Walmer House and climbed the steps to the imposing Victorian front door and rang the bell. Annabel opened it.

"What can I do for you?"

"I'm Rick. I've come to drive you to Persia!"

Annabel's large blue eyes stared at Rick for a moment.

"Oh! Sorry I haven't got my contact lenses in. I didn't recognise you."

She was obviously very short sighted. She let Rick into the hall and called to her mother:

"Rick is here."

"Who is Rick? What is he doing here?"

Road trip Isfahan 1969

A tall woman wearing reading glasses on the bridge of her nose joined Annabel. She stared severely at Rick and frowned. Her grey hair was scraped back and held in a bun.

"What do you want, young man?"

"I'm Rick."

"That I gathered."

"Annabel and I are going to drive out to Persia, tomorrow."

"Annabel! Did you tell me about this?"

"Yes Mum! You know I did! Really Mum, your memory is getting worse and worse!"

"Where do you live? You're not planning to stay the night, are you?"

Annabel answered for Rick: "Yes Mum! Of course, Rick is going to stay the night. He has come a long way. We will be gone first thing."

"Well, I've got work to do."

The eminent professor of English Literature returned to her study. Elizabeth Adams was an authority on the plays of the sixteenth and seventeenth centuries; she often seemed to confuse her children with characters from one of Marlowe's plays, as Annabel told Rick later. She didn't seem upset by her mother's bizarre behaviour. She smiled at Rick and asked: "Have you got an overnight bag or something? I'll show you the spare room, and you can rest up until supper."

Rick sat on the bed and looked around. He had never seen anything like it. His own home was kept neat and spotless by his house-proud mother, reflecting bourgeois values. Values he was struggling to reject. The decor here was Bohemian. He was anxious to fit in, but not

Road trip Isfahan 1969

sure what that might involve. Damp and decay oozed from a corner of the ceiling. The curtains were faded dark blue velvet, and there was a thick layer of dust on the windowsill. The view from the window looked out over a garden of lawn and flowerbeds that looked equally neglected. The house took second place to the life of the mind.

He wondered when supper would be; he didn't feel like reading so he decided to explore. The bathroom looked Edwardian, the basin had fine cracks in it and the taps dripped, but more off-putting was a line of cigarette ends around the bath. Rick relieved himself and pulled the chain: the sound of a tremendous torrent of water rushing out of the high cistern was followed by the most alarming clanking and hissing noises. He retreated downstairs looking for Annabel; he found her laying the table for supper.

"Can I help?"

"No. You don't know where anything is."

Rick did not argue, he stood and watched as Annabel went about her duties. There was not a word spoken. He wondered what she was thinking, she did not seem particularly glad to see him. He covertly admired her slight figure under her short blue summer dress which had a pattern of tiny pink roses. She tossed her head as she checked the table, her blonde ponytail swung from side to side. They moved into the kitchen, Annabel got a casserole out of the oven. She took off the lid and stared at the contents, poking about with a fork.

"I think it is done," she announced. "Ring the bell."

Rick looked helplessly around for a bell. Annabel pushed passed him, got hold of what looked like a

Road trip Isfahan 1969

curtain cord and pulled it. She opened a tall cupboard, took out four cold plates and started dishing out the stew. Her mother and her brother, Tom appeared and picked up a plate each. Rick copied, following them into the dining room.

"Where's the bread Annabel?"

"Get it yourself, Tom, you lazy hound."

Tom was in his second year at university, and about a year older than Rick.

"What do you hope to achieve by driving out to Isfahan?"

"I just thought it would be interesting, new places, new people, that kind of thing." Rick was on the defensive.

"Hot, dusty and boring. You two could learn more by staying here and reading the National Geographic."

Annabel butted in: "That's your opinion, but for me it is all about seeing the ancient world for myself."

Annabel was in her first year at St Hilda's, reading 'Greats'.

Tom was still on the attack: "How good a mechanic are you? Can you change a tyre?"

Rick was saved by Elizabeth telling Tom to get the pudding out of the fridge. Tom slouched off and then started shouting:

"What am I looking for?"

"Go and help him Annabel; men are quite useless, bring the yogurts and don't forget spoons."

"Spoons are already on the table, Mum."

Annabel stomped off to sort out her brother. Rick was only too grateful when the meal came to an end and he could retreat to his room for an early night.

Road trip Isfahan 1969

Next morning, he was first downstairs. He sat at the kitchen table and wondered where Annabel was; her mother appeared, her grey hair still up in a bun but wisps had escaped and hung down in disarray. She was smoking a cigarette in a black holder. After a lot of rummaging about she found some cereal and milk.

"We don't normally do breakfast in this house; help yourself."

Rick took a generous amount of Rice Krispies; they had obviously been in the cupboard some time because they had lost their snap, crackle and pop. He had finished them by the time Annabel appeared carrying a mountain of camping gear. Rick jumped up and helped her out to the Land Rover. It was no use pointing out that they were duplicating things. Annabel wanted all her own stuff.

"You don't need to bring a tent; mine is quite large enough for two people and Jon will have his own."

"Have you got a lamp? I have one that runs off camping gas and it's really good."

"OK, that'll be useful."

She went back indoors and reappeared with an enormous suitcase. Tom and Elizabeth appeared and watched as Annabel climbed up onto the bench seat. Rick started the engine. At this point her mother came around to the driver's side:

"Don't let Annabel drink any water that has not been sterilised, or sleep on damp ground."

"Of course not, we have Steritabs."

He noticed that the family did not show any emotion or kiss Annabel goodbye, even though they were obviously anxious. He engaged the clutch. For his part, he was just grateful to be on the road.

Road trip Isfahan 1969

Chapter Two
Oxford to the Dordogne

Rick was proud of the Land Rover with its white roof and sun-visor. The bodywork was light blue. What with the extra fuel cans and water carriers strapped to the front bumper, it looked the part.

"Can you map read?" Rick asked.

"Of course!"

"Then perhaps you could be the navigator?"

"Do you have a map?"

"Well, no. You'll have to use the AA Road Book."

Driving through London was not too tricky; the traffic was light and the South Circular road well signposted. The leafy suburbs of Bromley were soon behind them and the farms and oast houses of Kent rolled by. In Dover, the sky was overcast and the town appeared damp and drab. They had some time to wait for the ferry, so they went shopping: Annabel bought flip-flops, from a shop that sold buckets and spades.

"That's not very practical footwear Annabel! You need something to protect your ankles against snake bites."

"There are no snakes where we are going, and these are ideal for a hot climate."

-§-

At last they boarded the ferry to Ostend. There was a counter selling snacks in the main saloon. They sat down at a table by the window looking out over the promenade deck to the sea. Rick bought Annabel and himself cups

Road trip Isfahan 1969

of tea and slices of fruit cake wrapped in cellophane. She looked suspiciously at the cake.

"Railway cake," said Rick "It is really quite nice."

"Never seen anything like it!"

They got to discussing the next leg of the journey.

"I assume Jon told you that he expects us to pick him up from Carsac, in the Dordogne?"

"NO! When did he say that?" Annabel was aghast.

"Oh, I thought he kept in touch with you?"

"No."

"Well he wrote to me from the Dordogne to say he wasn't able to meet us in Ostend and I agreed to collect him from the archaeological dig in Carnac."

"Then why didn't you change the ticket to Dover/Calais?"

"It was a non-refundable ticket, and anyway it was too late by then."

"But the Dordogne is hundreds of miles out of the way!"

"Not really, in the grand scheme of things, and anyway I wanted to see that part of France."

"But why didn't you phone him and tell him to meet us in Germany? Why didn't you phone me?"

"Jon said in his letter that there was no phone at the farm, and I don't know your number. It only happened in the last week and I was so busy getting ready, organising visas and travellers' cheques."

Annabel was quiet, leaving Rick not only feeling foolish but also let down by Jon.

After a while he said: "I thought Jon was your friend. He organised the whole trip. I am just the driver. After

Road trip Isfahan 1969

we came up to Oxford to see you last term, I assumed he would keep everyone informed."

"Jon and I went to the same school, but he's two years older than me, so I don't know him that well. He gave me the impression that you were the organiser."

"So he didn't tell you that Sam is going to join us in Thessaloniki? She decided at the last minute to go to an archaeological dig in Crete."

"No. He didn't say anything about Sam, I assume she is his new girlfriend but I don't know her at all and didn't even realise that she was planning to join us. She's from Birmingham, isn't she?"

"I don't know. I met her in Culloden Hall when Jon brought her to supper. They are in their first year at the Institute of Archaeology. It was Jon's idea for us to drive out to the dig at Baba Jan."

"Oh God!" exclaimed Annabel.

Rick left her and went up on deck. The white cliffs of Dover had receded into the mist long ago. Rick felt sad and anxious. He leant against the rail, when would he see England again? He thought about his mother and sister back in the neat little cottage in Hampshire, very different to Annabel's home. His mother had helped him pack all the camping gear into the back of the Land Rover, even making sure he had enough cutlery and a can opener.

An announcement for drivers to re-join their cars came over the loud speaker. He returned to the saloon and together they went down to the car deck.

"We should get as far as Rouen this evening," said Rick.

Road trip Isfahan 1969

Annabel blinked and shook her head. "We will be turning back on ourselves. We could have saved a lot of time and expense if we had changed the ferry ticket to Dover/Calais," she repeated.

Ostend was cloaked in fog and rain. Annabel asked for the map and Rick had to confess he had no map that covered Ostend to the border.

"My plan was to turn right and keep going."

To their mutual surprise the plan worked. They were soon across the border and in France. Annabel took charge of the Michelin Map of Northern France. She turned out to be good map reader.

"Annabel, be a bit careful of the map; it is the only one we've got and there's a long way to go!"

"Just drive."

Driving in the rain and fog was not easy. They sped through one village after another and came to Deauville. By now they were exhausted and hungry. Annabel broke the silence:

"Let's stop and find a restaurant."

Rick was only too willing to oblige. They soon found themselves seated in a cheerful café/bistro, with red and white checked tablecloths. Annabel was fluent in French and ordered steak and chips for them both. The waiter seemed to equate being able to speak French with being good at making love, from what little Rick understood.

"What did he say to you? I failed 'A-level' French."

"He seems to think we are a couple on honeymoon. He said something about steak being good for lovers."

Annabel did not smile. The meat was in a peppery sauce; it was quite tough.

Road trip Isfahan 1969

"Horse meat, I expect," said Annabel in response to Rick's comment.

His alarm and surprise at this piece of information made her laugh: "Didn't you know? They eat horses in France."

"No, I didn't! I wish you hadn't told me."

It was getting late and the weather had not improved. They left the restaurant and headed westwards towards Rouen. It was now dark and hope of finding a campsite faded. Eventually they stopped by the roadside on a wide verge and made camp.

"We could have planned this a lot more carefully," said Annabel. "There is a Michelin guide you know."

"No, I didn't. When we go on holiday we just camp in a farmer's field. Farmers are generally very obliging."

"But in France?!"

There was no answer to that and Rick erected the tent as best he could on the wide verge.

"Are you going to sleep in the tent, Annabel?"

It was still raining, the tent was leaking and as the ground sheet was not sewn in place, puddles formed in all the depressions. She crawled inside.

"Oh damnation! My dress is getting soaked." She glared at him, took her sleeping bag and made herself as comfortable as she could on the front seat of the Land Rover.

Rick felt a wave of homesickness; he imagined Annabel was feeling a bit anxious too.

-§-

Road trip Isfahan 1969

Farm labourers woke Rick at 4.30am, he crawled out of the tent and roused Annabel, who was sleeping soundly. The rain persisted so boiling a kettle was out of the question. For what seemed like ages, they drove towards Rouen looking in vain for a place to stop for a cup of coffee. Nothing was open. At last they came to a village that boasted a café. Annabel took charge and ordered café-au-lait and croissants. They used the washrooms and set off again in heavy rain. They reached a crossroads.

"Which way, Annabel?"

"No idea."

Rick took out the compass then headed southwest.

-§-

The cathedral at Rouen was dark and forbidding, but full of atmosphere. There was a wedding taking place. While Annabel watched the wedding party, Rick found the carving of Salomé carrying John the Baptist's head on a platter, which inspired Flaubert to write Trois Contes.

"Hey, Annabel, come and look at this."

"What is it Rick?" She didn't seem impressed.

"Well at last we have found something worthwhile. I thought you wanted to see the sights."

"See the sights! What a little tourist you are!" she said.

Rick was confused, after all, they were tourists.

They wandered around the town and found a boulangerie. The smell of freshly baked bread and croissants made his stomach rumble. Annabel asked the woman for a selection of pastries as well as a baguette.

Road trip Isfahan 1969

"No point in buying more bread, it will be stale by tomorrow. And anyway, I love shopping in France. Now to find an épicerie."

Rick was not sure what she was talking about, but hoped it had something to do with food. He was not disappointed, the store was full of strong smelling French cheeses with unpronounceable names, cured hams and other meat he had never even seen let alone tasted. With great confidence Annabel bought all they needed for the next few meals and he was impressed that she seemed to count every centime. They only had £50 each to last the whole trip[1].

Two hours and many miles later they picnicked on a farm track surrounded by fields of corn. It was still pouring with rain. They sat in the Land Rover and mutely stared out at the sodden countryside.

"I do so want to see the real France, Rick."

"We'll stop at Chartres, then. The cathedral is supposed to be even more beautiful than the one we have just seen."

When they arrived in the village the first things Rick pointed out to Annabel were the elegant flying buttresses and the monstrous gargoyles. The afternoon sun was shining through the stained glass of the west window in a magnificent array of red and green jewels. They wandered among the tourists. Guides were expanding on the art of the mediaeval masons and glaziers. Annabel seemed detached from the people around her, almost in a dream, she appeared happy at last. He stopped to take a photograph.

Road trip Isfahan 1969

"Only tourists take photographs; they don't have the imagination to see below the surface. You can't capture the magic of the cathedral in a picture. Imagine how it must have seemed to people in the Middle Ages. I would love to step back in time and witness a medieval baptism!"

Rick put the camera away. They left by the west door. A loud wolf whistle made them both turn towards scaffolding on the west side of the building. A man with a trowel in his hand waved at Annabel and smiled. He shouted something that might have been 'Hi darling!' in French. His mates laughed.

Annabel looked furious, Rick felt anxious.

"It's your dress, Annabel, I think the men can see right through it."

Annabel was wearing a light cotton summer dress in pale pink with a green leaf pattern. It was short but not too revealing until she was silhouetted against the sun.

"Nonsense, you should be standing up for me, not criticising."

Annabel seemed more offended by him than by the workmen.

"It's very suitable for a hot day in England," he said digging a deeper hole for himself.

They walked back to the car in silence.

Back on the road they crossed the Loire at Tours. The river and the ancient town looked very peaceful. Up river were the tall towers of a chateau high on a bluff, the windows ablaze in the light of the setting sun.

"There Annabel: the real France."

"No Rick, fairy-tale France. The real France is about the people, what they eat, what they smell like!"

Road trip Isfahan 1969

"Like the workmen on the scaffolding?"

"NO. Men are crude and smutty all the world over."

"French women are the real France then?"

"Now you're being silly, and I suspect you of having rude thoughts about French women. Men stereotype women and that is why they'll never understand us."

It was late when they eventually found a campsite. Rick pulled a towel and some shampoo from his bag and set off for the showers, Annabel trailed after him.

He realised something was wrong as soon as Annabel returned.

"You get the supper on and I will sort out the tent and the camp-beds."

"I can't do it, Rick. I am exhausted. I'm fed up and I wish I'd never come."

Annabel started to cry. Rick didn't know what to do. He stood beside her and patted her shoulder, feeling acutely anxious.

"You shouldn't have stopped me bringing my own tent. Yours leaks and is too small for the two of us. I've done lots of camping and it has never been a shamble like this. You're so hopeless; you don't have a clue. We are never going to get to Persia, Tom was right I should never have trusted you," she wailed between sobs.

Rick said nothing, but shifted from foot to foot. He tried to comfort Annabel but she pushed his hand away. She lit the stove and in complete silence, cooked sausages, beans and fried bread. She nibbled at hers and then gave up, climbed into the front of the Land Rover and slammed the door. Rick finished what was left, washed up and crawled into the tent.

Road trip Isfahan 1969

-§-

It was a glorious dawn. Rick made tea and handed a mug through the window to a horizontal Annabel. She had recovered her composure and was soon frying eggs for breakfast. Rick went off to shave and shower.

"Why do you bother shaving?"

"To keep up morale, Annabel."

"We are on holiday Rick, and nobody cares what you look like."

"Well then just for your benefit!"

Annabel rolled her eyes and looked grim. It was rather a quiet duo who drove towards Sarlat, which was the nearest town to Jon's dig at Carsac. At Annabel's suggestion, they left the boring main road and went down country lanes between small fields containing a few bony cows, to St Julien. They stopped for lunch by the side of a stubble field dotted with walnut trees. The meal consisted of a crunchy fresh baguette, coarse pâté and ripe, smelly cheese that they had bought earlier in the day; Rick found he was acquiring a taste for this sort of food.

"But for you, I would be starving to death by now, Annabel."

She looked at him suspiciously. "Don't you like Camembert?"

"Yes I do, and I'm glad you know what to buy." Rick said.

"Are you trying to make up for being so useless?"

"No. I really admire the way you're so confident in the shops. You know I'm no good at French."

Road trip Isfahan 1969

"Stop talking rubbish and let's go and see the caves. The Stone Age paintings should be interesting."

The caves at Lascaux were closed to the public. An extremely large man with a cigar was the official guide. The caves had been closed for six years, but he offered to show them around a rather disappointing exhibition.

"The paintings, which are unfortunately not on display, were made 17,000 years ago," he said in good English but with a comic French accent.

"The caves were shared with bears in ancient times when animals and men lived in harmony."

Before facing the others, they stopped off for a drink. Annabel was suddenly friendly and much less anxious now that they were nearly at the farmhouse where Jon and the other archaeological students were staying.

"I will say this for you Rick, despite all your short comings, you are a good driver."

"Anyone can drive."

"I can't. And so far, you've done OK."

They laughed about the fat man at the caves and his ridiculous stories about the cavemen living with bears.

-§-

Jon was standing outside the farmhouse when they arrived. Strolling over to the Land Rover, in his usual laid-back manner, he asked: "Did you two make out on the way down?"

Rick laughed, or rather snorted.

"I had thought when we all met up in Oxford that you two were made for each other!"

Rick shook his head.

Road trip Isfahan 1969

The archaeologists and their students were about to sit down to supper. Seated around the table were Jon's friends and colleagues. M. Bordes, who was in charge, had rented a farmhouse with enough bedrooms to accommodate all the students. Some of the students were from America, others from across Europe. Jon had clearly been making hay while Sam was out of the picture.

"Hi, I'm Lauren, from California, where are you guys from?" asked a tall blonde in tight blue jeans with spectacular flares.

She put her arm around Jon and kissed him.

"I'm Annabel and this is Rick. I'm from Oxford."

"Is he your guy, I mean boyfriend?"

They were both startled by the directness of the question.

"No, certainly not!" said Annabel.

"That was said with feeling," laughed Lauren.

The kitchen/dining area was in a great hall, with a long refectory table. Since it was a special occasion and the dig was drawing to a close, the wine flowed freely. Grant, a loud and overbearing American student, did a music hall turn which involved holding a bottle of wine between his legs and pulling out the cork accompanied by loud, rude, suggestive noises. Annabel laughed a lot and was clearly up for it when Grant suggested a trip to a club in Sarlat to round off the evening. She and Rick left the Land Rover behind and joined the others in two overloaded cars.

The club was dimly lit. Tables and chairs were in hidden corners, and sofas in alcoves. There was a dance floor in the centre of the room. Rick and Grant went to

Road trip Isfahan 1969

the bar to order drinks while Annabel went over to a sofa and sat down by herself. Jon and Lauren were nowhere to be seen. Rick leant against the bar and chatted to one of the guys who had been on the dig. The place was bathed in a blue haze. It seemed all the men and most of the women had a cigarette either between their fingers or hanging from their upper lip and by the smell, it was not only tobacco they were smoking. Dance music was playing in the background. Grant took a drink over to Annabel.

Rick got bored with talking to the stranger and wandered outside. Animal grunts were coming from a dark corner of the garden. He walked over to investigate; Jon's white bottom came into view, humping Lauren. The ridiculous sight was both amusing and disturbing at the same time. He retreated to the dance floor. The music was now much louder and faster, nearly all the rest of the party were jiving, something he had only seen in films. It looked complicated and he wondered if it was an American thing or if the students had learnt it from the locals. Feeling rather inadequate and missing Annabel, he went back to the bar. He noticed Grant leading her off into one of the darkest alcoves. He started to follow but then stopped himself. Time passed. The next thing he heard was a scream and Annabel shouting:

"Get off! Get off me!"

Then silence. Rick hurried around the dancers in the direction of the noise. Grant was almost lying on top of Annabel; he had one hand under her dress.

"Come on!" he was saying. "You know you want it."

They were lying on the sofa. She was struggling to get free.

Road trip Isfahan 1969

"Get off her!" Rick lunged forwards and tried to pull Grant off; he was too heavy, but grabbing his long greasy hair and jerking his head back worked and Annabel wriggled free. Grant fell over onto his side; he was clearly drunk or stoned or both.

"It's cool man! I didn't mean anything!"

"You bastard!"

"How was I to know she's your chick?"

Rick went to hit Grant but Annabel pulled him back. She took his hand and they ran out into the garden, bumping into Jon and Lauren coming the other way.

"You two are in a hurry; can't you wait?"

"Piss off, Jon."

They found a bench and Rick sat down beside Annabel. She was shaking. He put his arms around her and held her tight. Sweat was running down his face and his heart was pounding.

"I can't breathe," she said.

"Did he hurt you?" he asked.

"No, you're squeezing me too hard!"

"Sorry."

"I just didn't think he would do that! I was so shocked! But I am glad you turned up when you did. Thank you."

Annabel turned towards Rick and smiled.

"You guys alright?" It was Jon. He was standing over them and looked concerned.

"Yes, we're alright now. Grant tried it on with Annabel. It all got a bit heavy but it's sorted now. We just want to go back to the farmhouse. It's been a long day."

Road trip Isfahan 1969

Annabel said nothing. Jon suggested he drive them back in one of the cars.

"I'll come back for the others later."

"Thanks mate."

Jon drove them back to Carsac. He showed them up to a room at the back of the farmhouse, with two single beds.

"You won't be disturbed here. Breakfast is at seven."

Jon left. Rick looked at Annabel and smiled. "I'll get your things from the car." He was back in five minutes, lugging Annabel's enormous suitcase and his own rucksack on his back.

"I didn't know what you might need so I brought it all. Do you want to go to the bathroom first?"

"No. You check it out. I don't want any more nasty surprises tonight."

Rick wandered down the corridor, thinking about what had just happened and trying to understand his feelings for Annabel.

"There's no lock. I'll be outside to make sure you're not disturbed."

"There is no need for that," she laughed.

Road trip Isfahan 1969

Chapter Three
Dordogne to Yugoslavia

It was rather a quiet bunch who came down to breakfast in the great hall, and tucked into sausages, tomatoes, bacon and eggs served on fried bread.
Annabel had coffee and a croissant.
"We are in France, you know!"
"Yes but there are so many English and Americans here that cook has agreed to do the real thing," Jon explained.
He was reading a letter, he looked worried, not his usual relaxed self.
"Sam says she will meet us in Marseilles."
"Great! Does she say when she will get there?" asked Rick.
"Today."
"Wow, we must leave immediately; it will take five or six hours to get to Marseilles."
"What are we doing? Where are we going?" asked Annabel.
"My girlfriend Sam is joining us in Marseilles.' Jon hesitated, embarrassed – a first for him. "She writes that she thought it would be better than waiting for us in Thessaloniki."
"And what about Lauren?" Annabel was not slow to realise the implications of Sam's unexpected arrival.
"What about me?"
Lauren, wearing a loose kaftan top and tight American blue jeans, arrived at the table just in time to catch her name.
"Ah," said Jon, and took Lauren back to their room.

Road trip Isfahan 1969

The scene that followed can only be guessed at. It was a subdued and tearful Lauren who returned. Annabel jumped up and hugged her. "Men are such bastards," she said.

Lauren managed a weak smile and nodded.

"Do you want something to eat?"

Lauren shook her head.

"Just coffee then?"

She sat down next to Rick.

"What are you going to do?" he asked. "Do you want to come to Marseilles?"

"No, I'll stay here, for now. I have to fly home soon anyway."

-§-

Jon came downstairs with his belongings in a rucksack, and got into the Land Rover without saying a word. Lauren turned and walked back into the farmhouse. Annabel ran after her and gave her a final hug.

"Goodbye Sarlat!" said Rick and away they went in a cloud of dust.

After Aurillac, Jon took over the driving, but almost immediately an argument broke out between him and Annabel. She was navigating and directed Jon down a narrow country road, lined by tall poplars. They got stuck behind a horse and cart, piled high with hay. In the fields, farm workers were loading the harvest onto similar wagons.

"Annabel, we really have to get a move on. We can't go bumbling along the scenic route."

Road trip Isfahan 1969

"Why not, Jon? We have plenty of time and the whole point of this trip is to see something of the countries we are passing through."

"No. No Annabel. We must get to Marseilles tonight, or Sam will be on her own."

"What about Lauren? Won't she be a bit lonely?"

The Land Rover swerved round a bend on the wrong side of the road.

"Jon!" Annabel screamed. "You'll kill us all, let Rick drive."

Rick had never heard her sound so angry. Jon stopped in the entrance to a field and they changed drivers. Annabel directed Rick towards Valence, and pointedly refused to talk to Jon. Rick dreaded Annabel's outbursts even though this one was aimed at Jon. So, when she turned and beamed at him he felt relieved.

They crossed over a river. Rick stopped the Land Rover in a meadow, and announced a lunch break. The river flowed into a pool, partly screened by trees. Annabel got out crusty French bread, tomatoes and cheese that even in the open air smelled ripe.

"Come on Annabel, let's have a swim before we eat."

She looked at Rick in her short-sighted way and smiled. They took their towels and ran down to the water. There was no one about and Jon had wandered off. As if throwing down a challenge she turned away from him, slipped out of her dress and plunged stark naked into the pool. Rick stared after her, hardly registering what he had just seen. He hesitated and then followed her example.

Road trip Isfahan 1969

"Let's pretend this is Grantchester and you're Virginia Woolf!" he called, suddenly feeling confident.

"I can't think of you as Rupert Brooke! You are much too boring!"

"Thanks!"

He tried to grab her leg but she was already swimming away. Getting out first, he pulled on his shorts, and gallantly handed a towel to Annabel as she emerged from the water. She held her arms across her chest and fixed him with her startling blue eyes.

"Don't look and hold the towel around me while I dress," she commanded.

As she wriggled into her clothes he admired her curiously striped back and bottom, marks left by sunbathing in a variety of costumes.

"You look like a zebra," he unwisely volunteered.

Without the slightest warning, she slapped him across the face. He blinked and tried to catch her wrist before she hit him again but she was too quick and darted away, bubbling up with laughter.

"I told you not to look!"

"But you're a beautiful zebra."

"But I've got a face like a horse, that's what you're saying!"

"OK, panda then, a beautiful panda."

"Now I'm fat like a bear!"

-§-

They crossed the Rhone at Arles and continued south east towards Marseilles. After two hours Annabel called a halt, and taking Rick in tow, went off to buy pâté,

Road trip Isfahan 1969

cheese, tomatoes, eggs and crusty baguettes for supper. The épicerie smelled of ripe cheese, cured meat and herbs, Rick wrinkled his nose.

"Look Annabel here is one called the feet of the English. Is that smelly enough for you?"

"Pié d'Angloys does not exactly translate like that Rick, but let's try it."

He pointed to a can of tomatoes on the top shelf and the girl came around from behind the counter, brushed past him and climbed onto a stool to get it down. When it came to paying, Annabel turned to Rick and told him how much cash to hand over the counter.

"Merci bien, Madam," Rick hazarded as they left the shop.

"You don't call girls Madam."

"She was pretty, but she did smell different, and for that matter, so did the shop."

"What are you on about?"

"You said we should explore the real France. I'm telling you that French girls don't smell like English girls. You, for example smell like a rose."

"I really don't know what to say. If you are trying to flatter me you're wide of the mark."

"But why do French girls smell different?"

"Perhaps because they don't have proper bathrooms."

Rick considered this bald statement, in the context of the arrangements at Walmer House, opened his mouth, then thought better of it and closed it again.

"Now you look like a goldfish! Were you going to say something?"

"No, Annabel."

Road trip Isfahan 19

She walked on in front of him; he watched the sway of her hips.

"I thought she smelled rather nice," he ventured.

"Keep your animal thoughts to yourself."

"You look quite fit, for an academic."

Annabel looked at him over her shoulder and started laughing.

"Race you," she called, and set off at a sprint.

Rick was disadvantaged by the shopping but he still managed to overtake her before they got back to the others.

"You wouldn't have caught me if I hadn't been wearing flip flops."

He smiled.

-§-

At last they got to Marseilles and made their way to the Youth Hostel that Sam had described in her letter. There she was sitting on the steps with her rucksack packed and ready to go. Rick was so pleased to see her again. She looked stunning. She wore a long light grey shirt over dark grey shorts.

"You're so brown! You look incredibly fit!"

Her curly dark hair hung loose to her shoulders. She greeted Annabel, and then Jon came forward to be hugged and kissed. Rick watched their reunion anxiously, wondering if Sam would sense anything different about Jon. Sam obviously suspected nothing; Jon was clearly an expert at deception. Sam got in the back and sat on the luggage. Jon climbed in with her.

Road trip Isfahan 1969

In a field by a stream they stopped for the night. Sam put on her bikini and she and Rick swam. They were old friends and Rick did not feel that he had to impress her or make clever remarks. He thought of Sam as an older sister and the fact that she was Jon's girlfriend made that all the easier. He knew she was not available and she didn't give him any encouraging signals. Annabel on the other hand was different. She didn't seem to have a boyfriend; at least she didn't talk about him if he did exist. Sometimes she seemed to be flirting; at other times she was openly hostile. He felt confused. He thought of asking her about boyfriends outright and immediately realised he would never be able to do that. When they were getting on well he was happy, when she snarled at him anxiety quelled all other emotions.

Annabel was preparing the evening meal when they returned from the stream. He went over and stood watching her stir the ratatouille.

"Can I do anything?"

"Get out the plates and cut up the bread," she said. "Please," was added as an afterthought.

"Is there anything to go with the ratatouille?"

"I'm going to do an omelette, and there is apple and cheese to have after that."

"Brilliant! What a feast and all on one burner. You're a great cook."

"Hardly, but needs must when the devil drives. Actually, I hate cooking."

Jon and Sam joined them. They were holding hands. Jon smiled at Annabel and said. "Rick is the devil then?"

"Saint or sinner it's all the same to me provided he does the driving and keeps us safe."

Road trip Isfahan 1969

"Harsh, Annabel. I think he is just lovely," said Sam.

Rick gave her a grateful smile; he could depend on her for support.

They sat down in a circle around the cooking pot and Annabel spooned out pieces of omelette and the stewed veggies. There was complete silence as they ate, but after a couple of bottles of the local wine, they all relaxed.

Jon got out his guitar and sang: "If you are going to San Francisco."

The irony was not lost on Rick, but Sam suspected nothing.

The boys washed up in the stream, and the atmosphere was very pleasant until it came to pitching the tent. There was something wrong with the way the ground sheet was arranged, and Annabel got cross; she picked up her wash-bag and towel and headed for the stream.

"Just sort it! I won't be long."

They wrestled the tent into some sort of shape with the ground sheet pegged down inside.

"Here we go again!" Rick muttered. "One minute she is the naked Venus and the next a witch out of Macbeth."

Jon laughed.

"What are you laughing about, boys?" Annabel emerged from behind the bushes.

"You are a real sport, Annabel," said Rick. "Not many girls would put up with such primitive arrangements."

At last all was peace and quiet: Annabel and Sam slept in the tent, Jon and Rick on the camp-beds set up beside the Land Rover in the open. He lay on his back

Road trip Isfahan 1969

staring up at the sky, identifying the different constellations.

"Wow! Look at that!"

Jon mumbled: "Specs!" and fumbled about until he found them; the heavens were alive with shooting stars. The meteor shower died down and Jon started to snore, but Rick stayed awake thinking about Annabel. He pictured her stepping out of her blue dress and swimming away from him. He drifted off to sleep and in his dreams, she turned into a tiger and was about to maul him; he tried to run, but panic took over and he felt himself falling. Now wide awake he smiled: she's one scary female, he thought.

-§-

Rick was up first, then Annabel appeared and bustled about with her usual efficiency: hard boiling eggs for later while making tea and packing up all at once. He smiled at her and for one crazy moment wondered if she knew he had dreamt about her.

"You can be in my dream if I can be in yours," he murmured in a poor imitation of Bob Dylan. "Do you dream Annabel?"

"Not last night, I slept like a log."

Rick was disappointed. He'd wanted her to say something less prosaic. They packed up and headed for the pass at Montgenevre. The scenery was wild, romantic and inspiring: steep rocky gorges and wild torrents. A winding road led to the top of the pass, and at every turn there was a fresh view of magnificent snow-covered mountains. Every so often they passed a group

Road trip Isfahan 1969

of climbers carrying ropes and ice axes on their way down from the peaks and glaciers.

"I've climbed in North Wales," said Rick.

"The Alps are a bit different I would imagine," said Sam.

"Yes," Rick continued, "there is nothing like clinging onto a sheer rock face by the tips of your fingers to make you feel alive. No worries about being mistaken for a tourist in that situation."

"But that is exactly what these climbers are!" Annabel butted in. "They're not experiencing any real emotion at all, just cheap thrills."

"Now you sound like your brother!"

"Children, please calm down!" Sam shouted from the back. "You two squabble like twins."

Annabel and Rick exchanged looks, eyebrows raised. For a while they drove in silence.

"Puis-je avoir vos passeports, s'il vous plaît?" said the customs officer on the French side of the border.

"Passaporti per favore," said his Italian counterpart.

They complied with these simple requests. On top of this Alpine pass, the formalities were minimal. They followed the narrow winding road down a valley where pastures gave way to vineyards, the leaves of the vines already turning to gold. On the densely populated plain there was no secluded field where they could camp.

"I suggest that we stop at the next campsite."

"Yes, please stop soon, I need to stretch my legs," said Sam

"OK," said Rick "I'm looking out for one."

Road trip Isfahan 1969

"If you want a pee Sam, why don't you say so?" asked Jon. "Rick won't understand the urgency unless you use plain language."

Rick slowed down and turned off the road at a hand-painted sign that pointed to Camping. The site was basic: the farmer had put aside a small field and a barn for the campers, but there was a shower block. Sam hurried off. Annabel grabbed her towel and toiletries and followed.

"I am going to wash my hair," she told Rick over her shoulder.

He looked at Jon: "Do I need to know that?"

"She probably wants you to scrub her back."

"You and your one-track mind!"

Annabel cooked up some more ratatouille to go with fried eggs, while the boys took their turn in the showers.

"Do you mind if Jon and I share the tent tonight?" asked Sam.

"Not at all. I'll sleep on my camp-bed in the barn," said Annabel.

"How are you and Rick getting along?" Sam thought Rick was out of earshot but she had miscalculated.

"Well, the jury is still out. At first I thought a bit of a prat, but I'll reserve judgement for a while longer."

"He improves on acquaintance; I think you'll find."

They laughed. Rick smiled to himself. If he had been wondering what Annabel was thinking, he now had it from the horse's mouth, no need to despair.

Rick and Annabel put up their camp-beds in the barn. They had the place to themselves. There was a thunderstorm in the night and torrential rain.

"Are you awake Annabel?"

"Why? Are you afraid of the thunder?"

Road trip Isfahan 1969

"No. I just wondered if you wanted me to hold your hand?"

"Don't get fresh with me Rick; you'll regret it!"

"Just being brotherly, Annabel."

"Another brother is the last thing I need."

"Goodnight, Annabel."

-§-

Next morning with Rick at the wheel they followed the main route that ran along the southern shores of the lakes, in the wide flat Po valley. The roads were crowded with fast moving traffic. Italian drivers do not take prisoners: they just lean on the horn and keep going. Rick shot through a red light and narrowly missed a lorry, forcing it to break hard. Annabel remained surprisingly calm. Sam was having an argument with Jon about the exchange rate and did not seem to notice. Then, taking advantage of the motorway, they bypassed Milan and made good progress towards Lake Garda.

"Let's stop here," said Annabel.

"Why here?" demanded Jon, from the back.

"Because I am hot and tired and fancy a swim."

Rick brokered a compromise and they stopped at a taverna overlooking the water and views of snow covered alps in the far distance. The place was busy so for modesty's sake Annabel wriggled into a bikini. Sam and Jon did not swim but ordered wine and idly watched as Rick joined her. He dived for her legs but she was by far the better swimmer and easily escaped him. After pasta and a glass of wine, they continued towards Verona.

Road trip Isfahan 1969

"I love this town. I came here with my parents just a few years ago. It's the most romantic and civilised town in the world. The Roman amphitheatre is amazing."

"Annabel, you sound just like a tour guide."

"Sorry Jon."

"Well just don't lecture us, I am not a complete ignoramus."

They sat down outside a café by the river Adige upstream of the Ponte Pietra, and drank more wine. Annabel and Rick wandered off to look for Juliette's balcony, leaving Jon and Sam in an intense, private conversation.

They walked side-by-side, careful not to touch. Rick watched her out of the corner of his eye and caught her frowning slightly, as if in deep thought. They found the famous balcony and the square where Mercutio fought his fatal duel.

"I'm Romeo and you're Juliet?"

"No you're Mercutio, who plays the fool. A piece of acting that cost him his life," Annabel smiled at her own wit. A poster was advertising Nabucco: a performance was to take place that evening in the Roman amphitheatre.

"I'll take you to the opera," he said.

"Very gallant, but I expect you will still want me to pay for myself!"

"Yes, why not? Otherwise my £50 will soon be gone."

"Practical, but not romantic."

There was just the suggestion of a smile around her eyes, but Rick could not work out if she was teasing him. Did she want him to be romantic?

Road trip Isfahan 1969

§

Dusk found them seated high up in the amphitheatre. Rick sat close to Annabel, the evening breeze wafted her perfume towards him. Sam was on the other side, leaning against Jon. As it grew dark every person in the audience lit a candle and far away at the bottom of the enormous auditorium the performance started. The entrance of the Babylonian general, as he rode a real horse onto the stage, provoked a murmur of delight from the crowd who did not wait for the interval to show their approval. In fact, they were so bound up in the performance that at the end of each of the famous arias they started shouting, "Bissata!" The singer obliged by starting over again from the beginning. In the interval, the audience burst into song themselves: Va pensiero. When they had finished, they sang it again.

"By the waters of Babylon we sat down and wept." Annabel translated for Rick's benefit. "We are on our way to Babylon," she added.

"It's a good omen don't you think?" Rick touched her hand but she didn't respond, he never dreamed that one day he would indeed melt the ice maiden's heart.

-§-

Driving out of Verona they came to a campsite behind a petrol station.

"Save water and shower with your steady?" Rick invited Annabel.

Road trip Isfahan 1969

"Not today thank you."

There was only one shower so Annabel and Rick took turns. After supper, they sat around Annabel's camping gas light in a circle and Sam and Jon got out their guitars and sang the old favourites: songs by Woody Guthrie, Leonard Cohen and Bob Dylan. Annabel leaned against Rick and for a moment he relaxed. Her touch, even though it was only her shoulder against his, made him feel at peace with the world. Maybe this is happiness, he thought.

-§-

They carried on towards the border and after driving all day decided it was too late to cross into Yugoslavia. Up a track, past fields full of vines in neat rows, was a rather dilapidated farmhouse, surrounded by sheds, a chicken-run and a barn on stilts. An old woman came out and Annabel started talking to her in Italian.

"What's she saying?" asked Rick.

"I think she's summoning her daughter."

A girl about Annabel's age emerged from the shadows. She smiled and started talking French but even Annabel could not understand her. Annabel smiled back and answered in Italian.

"She's saying she has eggs and bread."

Jon looked bored.

"We must pay her," said Rick.

Annabel turned back to her Italian friend. There was more smiling and gesturing and talking in foreign tongues.

"What does she want now?" asked Jon.

Road trip Isfahan 1969

"She wants us to come inside and eat in the kitchen," said Annabel.

Annabel arranged the camping gas cooker on the windowsill. Rick was outside passing aubergines, tomatoes and courgettes in through the window for the ratatouille. The girl's mother, or she could have been the girl's grandmother brought out an earthenware jug of wine.

"I did offer to pay for the food and wine but the girl seemed quite offended," said Annabel.

"Well you tried. And they seem very happy to have us," said Rick.

After supper Annabel and Rick curled up in the Land Rover, she on the front seat and he in the back; while Jon and Sam enjoyed the luxury of the tent.

"Good night Annabel!"

"Night, night!"

Rick nodded off, dreaming of Annabel. They were clasped in each other's arms, rolling down an endless grassy bank. He tried to kiss her but she wouldn't stop laughing. They were woken by cocks crowing and church bells ringing. A light rain began to fall.

Road trip Isfahan 1969

Chapter Four
Yugoslavia to Thessaloniki

Crossing the border into Yugoslavia went without incident.

"I hate these main roads, Rick. One of these lorries could run us off the road at any minute."

"Your right, Annabel. We will get onto minor roads just as soon as we can."

They spent the next two days bumping along dirt tracks to Dubica, where they stopped to stock up on bread, butter (which melted straight away) cheese, grapes and wine. The bread was leathery and dark brown in colour:

"Peasant bread," commented Rick, "God knows what it is made of!"

"It's certainly organic, it will do us all good," said Sam.

Annabel did not look enthusiastic but said nothing. They continued down what were basically farm tracks. As they rattled along they came across a band of Gypsies. Skinny ponies were pulling carts. They had three bears with them. Two bears were chained to the carts but a third bear was riding in a cart. More than twenty ragged children were playing a wild game of tag. Rick wanted to stop for a lunch break, but Jon and Sam were keen to press on.

The countryside was flat and featureless and it was a relief to at last arrive in Belgrade; the city was an interesting mixture of ancient classical buildings and modern concrete blocks. The cathedral was large and

Road trip Isfahan 1969

ugly compared to the ones they had seen in Northern France, with their elegant flying buttresses and wonderful stained glass. The interior seemed absurdly opulent and over decorated with angels and saints covered in gold leaf.

"Greek Orthodox?" Rick asked.

"Roman Catholic," said Annabel dogmatically.

"It could be a bit of both and may even have been a mosque at one time," said Jon.

"How do you mean?" asked Rick.

"In this part of the world the Ottoman Turks ruled for centuries, but the people were mostly Orthodox Christians, who were eventually liberated by Roman Catholic Archdukes from Vienna."

"A rich mix," commented Sam.

"Complicated," said Rick.

Annabel tossed her head as if to say she knew all this and resented Jon showing off. Sam and Jon stopped to take photos while Annabel dragged Rick off to buy supplies of leathery bread, goat's cheese, wine and vegetables.

That evening found them in a pleasant field with a stream running through it. Rick and Jon pitched the tent, Annabel and Sam started cooking vegetables and spaghetti for supper.

"Is that a two-girl job?" asked Jon.

"Is what a two-girl job?" responded Sam.

"Cooking."

"No," said Sam. "But I can see that you two boys need help putting up the tent."

The place was not as deserted as it first appeared. There was a crashing in the bushes and a drunk

Road trip Isfahan 1969

wandered into their campsite. In whining tones, he started begging.

"What's he saying, Jon," asked Sam.

"Haven't a clue," said Jon making gestures at the tramp that were supposed to mean what do you want?

The tramp gestured back, suggesting he was hungry.

"Oh goodness, Rick. Just make him go away," pleaded Annabel, positioning herself behind him.

"Ignore him and he'll go. Take no notice."

"Easier said than done, Rick," said Sam.

Things got even more threatening when two more men appeared but it seemed they knew the tramp and evidently told him to get lost because he disappeared. After a few friendly words in a language that Rick had never even heard before, the two men left. It started to rain.

"Let's get out of here. I don't want to be around when he comes back in the night," said Annabel.

"I agree," said Sam.

Jon shrugged.

"OK, let's go," said Rick and started dismantling the tent.

After what seemed ages they found a small rather dingy campsite which was home to some noisy but friendly dogs.

Annabel resuscitated the meal.

"You're a genius Annabel," said Rick

"What's that supposed to mean, Rick? I was as scared as you were. I don't know what we are going to do when we can't find a campsite in future."

"We'll be OK. We will check things out a bit more carefully before making camp, that's all."

Road trip Isfahan 1969

Annabel looked unconvinced. Rick took her wrist. "We're going to be fine," he told her.

-§-

Rick was up early. The sun was shining and the tent was drying out fast. He made some hot drinks.

"Rick!" called Annabel as he returned from the showers. "You're looking very smart, all freshly shaved."

"I do my best. I am trying to look as respectable as possible in the circumstances!"

In fact, his khaki shorts were rather crumpled and his blue Viyella shirt slightly grubby.

"My uncle who worked for Iraq Petroleum stressed that the tribesmen were more respectful if one was shaved and smartly dressed.

"I didn't know you had an uncle, let alone one who worked in the Middle East."

"Well I do. When Kurdish rebels took him from his house in Kirkuk, he changed into his best suit before agreeing to leave."

Annabel continued to fry the eggs without making a comment.

"How are we doing for food, Annabel?"

"We will have to stop in Skopje for the usual, a water melon would be good if we could find one."

-§-

Crossing the border into Greece was uneventful, just rather slow due to the number of lorries heading South;

Road trip Isfahan 1969

they pressed on towards Thessaloniki. They needed fuel, but it turned out to be ludicrously expensive: a gallon cost seven shillings and eight pence.

"What is the exchange rate?" asked Sam.

Annabel told her.

"The bastards cheated us," she said.

We need to be more careful where we fill up and where we change money," said Jon.

Rick didn't comment for once. His total concentration was on the road ahead. A battered Mercedes was overtaking a lorry, hurtling towards them on the wrong side of the road. Rick swerved out of the way. Annabel screamed. Jon laughed as they straightened up.

"You're lucky Rick's driving Annabel. He loves dicing with death."

"I do not!' said Rick

In Thessaloniki, the traffic slowed down but the drivers got even more aggressive, and it was with relief that Rick stopped on the edge of a park where hippies were camping. The four of them piled out of the Land Rover and stretched. They entered a café. The first thing Rick noticed was a girl holding her head in her hands, tears running down her cheeks. Sam and Annabel went over and sat down beside her while the boys hung back. She told them, between sobs, that all her money had been stolen from her bag while she was sleeping in the park. She finished her tale of woe by saying defiantly:

"I still mean to get to Istanbul."

Rick sat down beside Annabel.

"What's your name?" he asked.

Road trip Isfahan 1969

"Sue." She looked at him nervously and when Jon appeared, even more alarmed.

"It's alright, they're with us," said Sam.

"What's the dish of the day?" asked Jon.

Sue wiped her eyes with a napkin, "Cold fish in a tomato sauce with little green beans, I can't honestly recommend it," she said.

Jon ordered five kebabs and two bottles of retsina.

"That'll cheer you up," he said.

"We're on our way to Istanbul," said Sam.

"You can come with us if you don't mind sitting on the luggage in the back," Rick offered.

"That's kind of you but I need to go to the Police and after that to the British Consulate to sort out the business of my stolen money," Sue said. "It is going to take ages and I don't want to hold you up."

"We could lend you some money," said Annabel, to Rick's alarm and surprise.

"You're sweet, but I've got to go now."

She wandered away into the night.

They paid the bill and set off to look for a campsite. What with the exertions of the day and the retsina they got lost. Eventually they found somewhere run by an old Greek gentleman. He spoke fluent French but no English. Annabel was in her element.

"You are amazing Annabel," Rick said. "Where would we be without you?"

Annabel smiled her sweetest smile. Rick climbed into his sleeping bag in the back of the Land Rover grinning, but not knowing why. Sam and Jon continued to occupy the tent in domesticated bliss, or so Rick assumed until shouts roused him just as he was slipping

Road trip Isfahan 1969

into oblivion. He lay still, listening for a while and then sat up, there was a rumpus going on in the tent.

"You total bastard! Why did I ever think I could trust you?" Sam shouted.

Jon was trying to calm her down: "It's not perfume, it's aftershave! I started wearing it because the washing facilities were so primitive in Carsac."

"Do you think I am a fool? This is Chanel No 5. It's a girl's perfume and it's all over your T-shirt. I saw you furtively smelling it, you little pervert."

"At least it's not her knickers," Jon countered.

Bad move, thought Rick, anticipating bloodshed.

"You disgust me," Sam screamed.

Annabel was sitting up now and staring over the back of the seat at Rick who stared back not sure what to say.

"Aren't you going to do something?"

"Me?"

Struggling out of his sleeping bag and into his shorts, he cautiously approached the tent. Annabel didn't move.

"Er, are you guys alright?"

Sam emerged from the tent wearing nothing but a T-shirt and pants, but still managing to look like one of the Valkyries. Her eyes were enormous and her hair swirled around her head in a storm of black curls. She seemed to be about to run off into the night. Rick put his arms around her and held on to her. "Don't go."

"Let go of me! I'm only going to have a pee, you fool!"

Jon emerged from the tent looking shaken and sheepishly asked: "Can I move into the Land Rover?"

Road trip Isfahan 1969

Annabel took charge. "I'll move into the tent with Sam and you and Rick can sort yourselves out."

The boys climbed into the Land Rover. Rick did not dare break the silence; he drifted off into an uneasy sleep, imagining he could hear the girls plotting in the tent.

Road trip Isfahan 1969

Chapter Five
Thessaloniki to Istanbul

Next morning, he was up early, made tea and shaved. It was a ritual that was comforting at such a stressful moment and it gave him time to think, away from the others. He was not sure what would happen if Sam refused to forgive Jon. It could be very awkward. If Jon left on the other hand, perhaps Sam would not want to continue to Persia, and then she and Annabel might demand to be taken back to England. The whole thing seemed a mess. The girls were up when he got back and Annabel had made breakfast for all of them except Jon who was pointedly excluded.

"Let's go back into Thessaloniki, and have coffee and baklava." Rick suggested.

Annabel smiled. "What a good idea, Rick. I'll help you pack up."

She seemed to be expecting him to take the lead and keep the show on the road. Jon climbed into the front seat and the girls sat in the back, conspiratorially. Rick headed back into the centre of town and stopped outside the kebab shop they had visited the day before. All four sat down around a table on the pavement, the atmosphere was awkward.

"Come on, Rick," said Annabel, she stood up.

He followed her out of the shop. She put her arm through his and pulled him along without saying anything until they were round the corner. "Can't you see they need to be alone?"

"Good thinking, Annabel, but I just can't guess what poor Sam must be feeling."

Road trip Isfahan 1969

"That's for them to sort out. Come on, I'm hungry."

She dived into a taverna. Rick sat down beside her and looked around. The place was empty but for two men at one end of the bar who were drinking a cloudy white liquid with the air of men who have nowhere to go. A waiter came over and Annabel ordered a doner kebab and Orangina. For once she did not order for them both. Rick was taken by surprise.

"Um, the same please," and turning back to her. "What do you think Sam will do?"

"If I were her I would kick him off the bus."

"And then what? He can't very well hitchhike home."

"Why not? Lots of people are doing exactly that."

They wandered back to the place they had left the unhappy pair. She was there but he had gone. She was crying silently; tears were trickling down her cheeks, a cup of coffee remained untouched. They sat down on either side of her and Annabel gave her a hug.

"What now Sammy?"

Rick had never heard Sam called that and marvelled at the way Annabel fell into the sister role. He wondered how Sam would react; she shook Annabel off and smiled grimly, and sniffed.

"He's gone to buy a ticket to Athens and from there take ship for Israel where he has a friend conducting a bronze age dig."

"Another bronze age dig?" asked Rick, "I thought the dig in Baba Jan was bronze age."

"That's irrelevant," snapped Sam. "The point is he's gone."

"Good riddance!" added Annabel.

51

Road trip Isfahan 1969

There was silence while they digested the situation. Rick ordered some beers.

"So, are we still on our way to Baba Jan?" asked Rick.

The girls stared at him.

"But of course; did you think we were going to chicken out just because the bastard has run away?"

-§-

They set off for Xanthi; the road ran between the sparkling sea and mountains covered in sunburnt scrub. Wild thyme was everywhere.

"Stop!" demanded Annabel

"We want to swim!" said Sam.

"I'm hungry," said Rick.

"You can eat later," said Annabel.

She did not risk going naked this time; the girls hid behind the Land Rover to change.

"Don't gawp!"

They performed a racing dive into the clear water. Rick watched them rolling over like seals. The girls started duck diving, coming back to the surface with water dripping from their earlobes like perfect diamonds. He stood still in the shallows, just watching, not wanting to break the spell. They turned and came racing towards him, and pushed him over as they ran up the beach.

"Out of the way, slow coach!"

He chased them back to the Land Rover, where they turned, at bay, like tigers. They crouched ready to spring. Rick tried to look cool. The girls laughed at him and between them managed to wrestle him to the ground.

Road trip Isfahan 1969

Rick had no idea what was going on. He escaped into the water to wash the dust off his skin. Once dry and dressed he climbed into the driver's seat and drove off. The girls jumped into the back and had to struggle into their clothes as the Land Rover rattled down the road. Sam started singing.

"We're all going on a summer holiday."

The other two joined in but the girls turned on Rick:

"You're so out of tune! Stop! Stop it!"

Lake Vistonida, stretched away for miles to a blue ridge of mountains; it seemed the ideal place to camp for the night. Before pitching the tent, they plunged into the warm translucent water. The sun was beginning to set and they seemed to be swimming in a silky rainbow of shimmering colours. Further up the shore a fisherman was casting a fly with long, lazy rhythmical strokes of his rod. The girls came back to the shallows and Annabel produced a bottle of shampoo. She poured some onto Ricks head and started to massage it in. He stood waist deep in the water and let her do it, tingling from his scalp to his toes. Sam watched for a minute, then dived and grabbed his ankles. He was tipped backwards onto Annabel who far from saving him pushed him under the water. He came up spluttering but the girls pushed him under again. He struggled onto the bank. "You meanies!"

The girls washed their clothes and hung their underwear and dresses out on a rose bush.

"Your dresses won't dry overnight, you silly things," said Rick.

The girls proved him wrong. By the time they set off again the next day their clothes were perfectly dry. It

Road trip Isfahan 1969

was not far to the border. The officials on the Turkish side were very slow, partly because they were hampered by some rather bedraggled hippies coming the other way who were being expelled from Turkey. The problem was that the Greeks did not want them either and they were trapped in no-man's-land.

"I don't like hippies," said Annabel.

"Neither do I," said Rick.

Sam looked at them in astonishment.

"What have the poor hippies done to offend you two little snobs?"

"Sorry Sam, I forgot you're a secret hippie."

The customs officer was beckoning them forwards.

"Wake up and stop blathering. It's our turn," said Sam.

They were waved through with minimal formalities.

The landscape was parched, the grass burnt by the sun and the few trees stunted and twisted by the climate. At last they found a track leading down to a headland. A Turkish family emerged from a cottage on the path to the beach. Rick tried to speak to them but they turned away.

"You're such a scruff, of course no one will talk to you if you look like a tramp," Annabel chided him.

"Thank you Annabel, but what am I to do? It is a bit late now to buy a new outfit."

Rick went off on his own to swim in the Sea of Marmara, while Sam and Annabel pitched the tent and made supper. Then it was the girls turn to swim while Rick watched over the ratatouille and opened a bottle of wine. It felt safe and the trio relaxed, sitting cross legged on the ground. Rick's fingers stroked the back of Annabel's hand and for once she did not withdraw it, she

Road trip Isfahan 1969

shuffled closer to him; they watched the sun sink into the sea.

-§-

"You're looking gorgeous! Where are you going?" said Rick.

The girls emerged from the tent looking very smart. They spent a few minutes organising Rick, in a clean shirt and Sam's tight white jeans. Sam made a habit of wearing boys' jeans so he looked almost respectable, ready to enter the ancient capital city of the Ottoman Empire. As Annabel climbed up into the seat beside him, Rick could not help noticing the tiny, fine fair hairs on her legs, only evident now that she was so tanned. Thinking about it made him smile. Her short summer dress left little to the imagination.

"You'll put on some trousers when we get into Istanbul won't you?" he tried to sound casual.

"Why? Is there something wrong with my legs?"

"Not at all, they're great legs."

Sam came to the rescue:

"This is a Muslim country and if we want to go into a mosque, we'll have to cover up. It would be better not to risk causing offence."

Annabel scowled but took the point and before they disembarked in front of the Blue Mosque pulled on a pair of jeans which she wore under her dress. She set off to inspect the place, Sam and Rick followed. They entered cautiously not knowing what to expect but were welcomed by an official who asked them to take off their shoes. He indicated a stall where they could buy

Road trip Isfahan 1969

headscarves. They covered their heads, and moved into the main body of the mosque.

"Wow! Amazing!" said Rick.

Above them were thousands upon thousands of blue tiles reaching up almost out of sight to the top of the dome. Most of the tiles were decorated with symmetrical patterns but some showed birds.

"Look at this carpet Rick," Annabel beckoned him over. She was gazing at a large green carpet from Abyssinia.

"What's so special about this one?

"It's green and the others are predominately red."

"It's different because it was made in Abyssinia and given to the Sultan by the Emperor," said the guide, making them jump; he had crept up behind them very quietly.

Annabel smiled at him, Sam came wandering towards them.

"Come on, time to go," said Rick.

"Why?" asked Annabel, as they walked away.

"Because I don't like the way that man is looking at you."

"What do you think he is going to do to her?" asked Sam.

"Did you think he might abduct me?" said Annabel.

"Well he might, you never know. People do just disappear."

There were more carpets in the Grand Bazaar. The smell of coffee, herbs, incense and cooking were overpowering. There was a general hubbub as if everyone was talking at once and no one was listening. The merchants kept up a persistent chatter aimed at

Road trip Isfahan 1969

luring tourists into their shops. Annabel avoided their gaze and kept moving, but Sam stopped and asked about some rings. She was instantly surrounded by eager salesmen. Rick kept very close to her but was now acutely aware that Annabel was moving out of sight. Sam bought two puzzle rings, while Rick kept peering about for Annabel. They found her a short while later in a shop drinking tea and talking in English and French to two bemused brothers about carpets.

"Annabel! I thought we'd lost you!"

"Why are you so anxious, Rick?"

"This man is your husband? He has lots of money to buy carpets?"

"No, he's my little brother and he's very poor, but I must go now and fetch my real husband, who will be delighted to buy your carpets."

The three of them turned to leave the shop but the brothers blocked their way.

"We take you to see our cousin. He has the most beautiful jewellery."

Outside the shop they quickly walked away, nodding and bowing:

"Thank you, thank you, but we really must go now!"

The Turks gave up. Rick and the girls hurried off but quickly got lost in the labyrinth of alleyways that make up the Bazaar. They didn't dare ask anyone. As they were hurrying along they almost bumped into a young man waving pamphlets. He looked about the same age as Annabel.

"Are you guys lost?" he asked in an American accent.

Road trip Isfahan 1969

"No, no. We are on our way to the Blue Mosque," said Sam.

"The Blue Mosque is that way," he said pointing back the way they had just come. He gave detailed directions and finished: "I am a student too. I will be going back to California next month!"

Hungry and tired they stopped in a café for doner kebab and coffee.

"There is no time to visit the Topkapi Palace now," said Rick, "but I promise we will on the way back."

Road trip Isfahan 1969

Chapter Six
Istanbul to Trabzon
Sea of Marmara to the Black Sea

"Where are we?" Rick asked Annabel who was sitting beside him map reading.

"Keep going straight ahead and we should find ourselves beside the Izmit Korfezi, or Bay of Izmit to you."

"So how far to Ankara?"

"About another 200 miles."

"So we won't make it tonight?" asked Sam.

"No chance," said Rick.

The wait for the ferry to take them across the Bosphorus meant it was already midday when they arrived in Asia Minor and darkness was falling by the time they found a place to camp on the shore. The ground was hard and the tent pegs buckled. The wick had burnt out in the lamp.

"Sod it! How can I cook in the dark?"

"Don't worry, Annabel, I'll get you a new wick as soon as we get to a town."

"It's not your fault Rick, it's just that I'm tired. Can you help by chopping up the onions?"

"Here, use my head torch."

They worked together in silence, Rick happy just to be close to her. Sam was busy reading by the light of a torch.

They were just finishing a bottle of wine when a man emerged out of the darkness and introduced himself as Mustafa Top. It turned out he was a student and his

Road trip Isfahan 1969

family owned a shop in Izmit. Annabel and Sam took turns to ask him questions using the Turkish-English dictionary. The three of them kept passing the book backwards and forwards so the conversation took a long time. Rick looked on anxiously, wondering where all this was leading. The upshot was that they exchanged names and addresses and agreed to meet Mustafa in the morning to take him to his parents' store.

"I don't think it will happen, do you?" said a sleepy Sam.

"You never know," said Annabel. "I thought he was really nice, and very trustworthy."

"I'm sure he fancied you. I wouldn't trust him at all," said Rick.

The sun was up and they were about to leave when Mustafa Top turned up with his gramophone and a basket of fruit and vegetables.

"Merhaba," said Sam. "Hello."

"Günaydin," said Annabel. "Good day."

Rick stared, trust the girls to be so friendly and to have taken the trouble to learn a few words of Turkish. Mustafa smiled broadly and answered their greetings with something that sounded quite elaborate. The only trouble was that the girls had completely exhausted their vocabulary and could only smile back at him.

"Sorry," said Rick, "we don't really speak Turkish."

Mustafa seemed to understand; he wound up his gramophone and put on The Best of the Animals. The girls got up and danced about like they were the audience on 'Top of the Pops.' To Mustafa they must have seemed quite exotic and for Rick the sight of Annabel in her short summer dress gyrating like Petula

Road trip Isfahan 1969

Clark on stage, made him want her more than ever. The record player ran down and to Rick's relief the girls stopped dancing before Mustafa could join in. The mixture of jealousy and anxiety was too much to bear.

"We've got to get a move on. Do stop gyrating about like Pan's People," said Rick.

"Spoil sport. What are you afraid of?" asked Sam.

All four of them climbed into the Land Rover. Annabel sat beside Rick; Sam and Mustafa shared the back. Sam could look after herself but Annabel was another matter; he felt a responsibility to protect her. They set off for Mustafa's shop in Izmit. The place was an Aladdin's cave of everything a household could possibly need to keep the lights on, the cooker working and the garden dug.

"What's this used for do you think?" Rick asked Sam.

She picked it up and turned it over. "It's an adze, used for shaping wood, I should think."

"How do you work that out?"

"You find them in archaeological sites where ship building was going on. Jon is into ancient tools." said Sam smiling.

Other strange implements littered the place; there was even a Post Office. Rick posted his cards and found an exercise book so that he could start a journal. Annabel selected a blue bead on a leather strap to ward off the evil eye and Sam picked up a set of worry beads. Mustafa would not let them pay for anything. They parted company with promises to write and visit. Annabel took a photo and off they went, heading towards Ankara on good fast roads, stopping only once

Road trip Isfahan 1969

in a village for the usual provisions: flat bread, wine, aubergines, tomatoes, olive oil and a watermelon.

"I need a pee," Sam announced.

"Wait till we are out of the village, then you can pee behind a bush," said Rick

"I'll keep you company," volunteered Annabel.

Late afternoon, about 60 miles west of Ankara, down a track that lead to a field by a river, they pitched the tent on the bank. Water buffalo were wading about downstream. After a swim, the girls washed their clothes.

"Can you rig a washing line for us please, driver?"

"No problem, ma'am."

Their light cotton dresses fluttered in the evening breeze. Two small boys cautiously approached out of the gloom and offered them some fish. They squatted on their haunches at a safe distance and watched Annabel preparing the meal. Evidently she was not that interesting because they soon disappeared back down the track.

"Shall I gut the fish or would you like to?"

"You do it, Rick. It's a man's job."

Once cooked, he scraped a tiny mouthful of white flesh off the bones and cautiously tasted it:

"Oh dear, it's just like a mouthful of cotton wool with pins in it!" he spat it out.

Annabel gamely ate a bit but Sam refused to try even a mouthful. They made do with bread and ratatouille and relaxed on cushions sharing the wine; one by one the stars came out. Rick sat close to Annabel; she leant against him.

"There is Orion, Ursa Major and the North Pole."

Road trip Isfahan 1969

Sam joined them, she started to yawn.

"It's been a long day. I'm off to bed."

Annabel joined her in the tent. Rick could hear them rustling about as they changed into night clothes. He lay on his camp-bed between the Land Rover and the tent. The girls were whispering; it was hard to make out more than the odd word. Then he heard Annabel say:

"Do you think he fancies me?"

"Of course he does."

"But you're the one he really likes, and besides you must have noticed how he looks at you. I wish I had big boobs like you, then he might look at me the same way."

"You're just talking nonsense. I've known Rick for years and we are old friends but you're the one for him. Boobs or no boobs," Sam said.

Rick suppressed a laugh. If only he could tell her how much he admired her slim figure, her big blue eyes, her dirty blond hair, her legs and…. and…. and. He went to sleep scheming how he was going to get Annabel alone so that he could tell her all this stuff.

-§-

In Ankara, they breakfasted off tea and baklava. The town seemed to consist of modern concrete buildings, there were no mediaeval alleyways like there were in Istanbul. The streets were crowded with people in Western dress; it felt familiar. Rick went off to find an ironmonger, hoping to get a replacement wick for Annabel's lamp. The other two went window shopping. When he got back to the Land Rover he found Sam reading Simone de Beauvoir's autobiography, and

Road trip Isfahan 1969

Annabel deep in an abridged edition of Sir James Fraser's "The Golden Bough".

"Two true blue stockings! What would your brother say if he could see you now?"

"He would wonder why I was sitting in Ankara when I could be on my way to the Black Sea," Annabel snapped her book shut. "Come on, get in and drive."

He climbed in beside her, for a moment their legs were touching, then she wriggled sideways.

"Get over!" said Sam. "You're pushing me out the door."

She pushed Annabel back towards Rick. He engaged the clutch and away they went, still jostling to get comfortable. The more Annabel bumped against him, the more aroused he felt. They were heading towards Samsun and the Black Sea. The day was hot, the countryside arid and the fields empty as the harvest had been gathered in weeks ago. A small boy and his mother were winnowing; the boy sat on a sledge, driving a donkey in circles over the corn. His mother tossed the straw into the air with a pitchfork to allow the grain to separate.

It felt that at last they were off the beaten track, but every time they stopped they were surrounded by children who begged for cigarettes, so clearly they were still on the well-trodden hippie trail from London to Katmandu. Sam tried to tempt the urchins with a healthy alternative, such as slices of watermelon.

It was part of the routine of the day that whenever they could they stopped for a swim. Every river was a chance to halt, swim and snack on watermelon while fighting off the cigarette demanding hordes of young

Road trip Isfahan 1969

boys. When the girls plunged into the water to wash their hair, the children were fascinated and cautiously tried to scoop up the foam. Rick felt anxious about pitching the tent beside the road, or even in a field out of sight.

"I want to avoid a repeat of the episode in Yugoslavia," he said.

"Quite," said Sam. "I certainly don't want any nasty surprises in the night."

The problem was solved that evening when they stopped for fuel. The people who owned the garage were very friendly and were only too pleased to show them a safe place to camp. Rick put up the tent using six inch nails instead of tent pegs, while Annabel cooked the ratatouille and Sam read her book.

"Where did you get those nails?" asked Annabel.

"Same place as I got a replacement wick for your lamp. Give me a mo. and I will put it in for you."

"You are a genius."

Annabel seemed so happy, it made Rick smile.

"Thanks Annabel! You're a great cook."

For a moment she held his gaze, Rick looked away, she seemed to be challenging him. He went to the Land Rover, got the map and laid it out on the rug. In the light of the lamp they lay beside each other and studied it. Sam came and lay down beside Rick so that he was now sandwiched between the two girls. This was the only map they had: it was printed on canvas and covered the whole of the Middle East.

"When was this printed?" asked Sam.

"It's right up to date: Bartholomew's World Series, 1967. It cost me seven shillings and sixpence."

Road trip Isfahan 1969

Annabel smoothed it reverently, as if to apologise for her earlier frivolous treatment of the charts. Rick watched her. The three of them traced their route to date and then discussed the next stage along the Black Sea coast. It looked as though the road ran a little way inland for some of the distance between Samsun and Trabzon. Sam lost interest in what Rick was saying and pushed him sideways into Annabel who reacted by pushing him back against Sam. He lay face down.

"Stop rolling me about girls, I am not Tom Kitten."

The girls giggled but said nothing. Then Annabel placed both elbows on his back and cupping her face in her hands, she stared at Sam.

"Leave him alone; he's mine."

She jumped on him, sitting astride him as if he were a horse. Sam hesitated only a moment before swinging a leg over so that she was sitting behind Annabel.

"There's room on your horse for two," she sang.

Rick was being squashed into the dirt, but the girls didn't seem to care, they started singing "Widecombe Fair", swaying backwards and forwards as if they were riding along on the grey mare in the song.

"I can't breathe," gasped Rick.

At last girls dismounted and convulsed with giggles disappeared into the tent. Rick pulled his camp-bed over to the side of the tent and lay down in his sleeping bag. He could hear scuffling noises as the girls got undressed and wriggled into theirs. He could indistinctly hear them whispering. So, agog to hear more, he stealthily moved his bed closer to the tent. Sam was asking Annabel if she fancied Rick? Annabel was being evasive and turned the

Road trip Isfahan 1969

question back to Sam. There was more giggling and then Sam's voice.

"You're committed now Annabel. You've made it so obvious that you fancy him."

"I'm not! I was only teasing and I'm sure he knows it."

Rick was not sure if her reply made him happy or sad, was she trying to hide her true feelings from Sam? Girls are an infuriating mystery, if only he could do something that would make her love him. He was drifting off to sleep when Sam emerged from the tent to go for a pee. She turned sharply right and fell over the camp-bed. It had not been there earlier. She tumbled right on top of the occupant.

"What are you doing here?" she shouted in his ear.

"Trying to get some sleep!"

"No you're not. You've been listening to us, haven't you?"

"No, no, not at all. And anyway, what could girls possibly have to say that would interest a bloke?"

Sam put her lips so close to his ear that he felt like he was being kissed.

"Well, suppose I told you that Annabel has the hots for you? Would that be interesting?" she whispered.

Rick turned to face her. Annabel joined the scene.

"What are you two doing?"

She burst into tears and ran off in the direction of the road. Sam jumped up and ran after her, followed at a safe distance by Rick. They caught up with her on the edge of the circle of light made by the lamps of the petrol station. Sam put her arms around her and held on

Road trip Isfahan 1969

tight. Rick stayed in the shadows. He could hear Sam but Annabel's replies were indistinct.

"Come on darling, I was only teasing Rick about his being so keen on you. I was whispering in his ear because I didn't want to wake you up."

Annabel raised a tear stained face and looked into her friend's eyes. She seemed so trusting that Rick longed to reach out and hold her.

"Rick really does love you, he's just told me so."

He moved closer so that he could hear her reply.

"Really? I thought I had caught you two kissing."

"No. Not at all."

Rick stepped out of the shadows.

"Annabel."

Sam slipped away. Rick and Annabel stared at each other then she turned and followed Sam.

"Good night, sweet thing," said Rick.

"I am not your sweet thing! I haven't made up my mind about you. I am going to sleep now. Don't get your hopes up."

She disappeared back into the tent, leaving Rick to lie awake all night trying to make sense of crazy, out of control feelings.

Road trip Isfahan 1969

Chapter Seven
The Black Sea

Next morning, they were up early and off before the sun came over the hill. Round a bend they came across more than half a dozen dead sheep in the road. A truck had recently run them over by the look of things. Their owners, dressed in long dark Biblical robes and wearing turbans were busy skinning them.

"Looks like there will be a spectacular feast in the village tonight," said Sam.

"I have been told that they eat everything including the eyeballs," said Annabel.

"And the bollocks!" said Sam.

The girls exchanged looks and giggled.

A huge truck came towards them on the wrong side of the road. Rick reacted instinctively and swerved into a field. They went bumping along for about a hundred yards and then regained the road.

"Lucky there are no hedges or ditches in this part of the world!" said Rick.

"Well done," said Annabel in awed tones. "We would have finished up like those sheep, if your reactions were a fraction slower."

Later that day they saw a horse that had been hit while pulling a cart. Its entrails were all over the road. Rick became even more cautious.

"I wish Jon was here to share the driving," said Sam. "It is a lot for you on your own."

Annabel put her hand on Rick's arm "It's a nuisance that neither of us can drive but I have every confidence in you. We're going to be just fine."

Road trip Isfahan 1969

Rick smiled at her.

"Keep your eyes on the road!" she said.

"It's a long way to go," Sam reflected.

They made it safely into Samsun and stopped for baklava and chai, in a basic tea house, just four bare walls and a dirt floor. There was a big samovar on a table, surrounded by small glasses and saucers. Annabel announced that she must have halva.

"What's halva?" asked Rick.

"Halva is a paste made of honey and sesame seeds."

"Wow! It sounds delicious."

All three left the shop and went from store to store looking for halva. But even when they found some it was not quite right and Annabel made them go on hunting until she found what she wanted. She haggled with the astonished shop keeper and eventually bought a kilo for six lira.

"We will be known around here as the halva addicts," said Sam.

The Black Sea coast was densely populated with villages and estates surrounding the villas of the rich and powerful, but they eventually found an isolated spot where a stream ran into the sea. The black sand was so hot that they hopped from foot to foot shouting: "Ouch, ouch, ouch!" They all plunged into the water. Rick and Annabel stood side by side and watched as Sam swam away, when he started to swim after her, Annabel jumped onto his back and they rolled over and over in the shallows. He tried to kiss her; she struggled free but as she did so her bikini top came undone. She stood stock still holding her arms across her chest, staring at him. She looked so fierce that Rick backed off. He did

Road trip Isfahan 1969

not see Sam emerging from the water behind him. The next minute he was on his back and thrashing about helplessly as she held him under.

"Don't molest my friend."

Rick spluttered and gasped:

"I wasn't, I was just … I was just…"

"Trying to kiss me!"

"No, No! I was just trying to see what it would be like to …"

"To what?" asked Sam.

"To kiss me!" shrieked Annabel.

The girls collapsed onto their knees in the water helpless with laughter. Rick beat a hasty retreat. When he returned to camp they were sitting side by side on his camp-bed with their backs to him. He moved forwards and paused. They had their heads together, whispering. He could hear the odd giggle and snort of laughter, but nothing very clear and then Sam said:

"Have you ever had a real boyfriend?"

"Well, no. Was Jon your first?"

"We are talking about you Annabel, why don't you let Rick near you?"

"Well, I'm not sure I want to go that far."

"You're afraid. That's the problem."

"No!"

"I think, in fact I know, that Rick has never had a real girlfriend, so he's probably even more anxious than you are."

"He certainly does seem a bit inexperienced, the way he tries to come onto me is quite funny some of the time."

Road trip Isfahan 1969

"You should just take the bull by the horns and do it!'

"What just like that? It might turn into an embarrassing farce. What if he doesn't get my drift?"

"He'll work it out, never fear. And you'll be fine, just so long as you love him enough to trust him."

"What shall I do then? I mean what should my opening gambit be?"

"Well, just mount him like you did just now, and I'll keep out of your way."

"How? I mean how is that going to work?"

"Well you'll have to turn him over first!"

The air was rent with squeals of hysterical laughter as the pair reflected on the image they had just created. Rick did not know what to do, he felt embarrassed by what he had just heard and yet at the same time quite aroused at the thought that Annabel fancied him. He stepped forwards. "Hello girls, I hope I didn't startle you?"

They turned and looked at him suspiciously.

"How long have you been there?" asked Annabel.

"Are you spying on us?" asked Sam.

"I was just walking up from the beach, I didn't hear a thing."

Annabel got up and stood in front of him, he thought she was about to say something important but apparently changed her mind.

"I'll put the supper on," she said.

The way she laughed as she said it made him understand that she was just a tease.

-§-

Road trip Isfahan 1969

Dawn was creeping out of the East, when they packed up and took the road to Trabzon. They had to stop for fuel; Sam got out the phrase book to ask the garage hands where to get tea and cigarettes. The guys misunderstood her and invited all three to sit down and share chai and a smoke. Their hosts invited them to taste raki and passed around small glasses filled with a clear but pungent liquid. It tasted quite strongly of pine needles and burnt all the way down, but was not unpleasant. They sat in a circle on cushions, the girls communicating with the Turks with the aid of the book.

Rick began to fear that soon they would be too drunk to move, and taking the phrase book away from Annabel, read out in Turkish: "We must leave immediately!"

The boss stood up, strode over to the Land Rover, and with a gallant bow, wrenched the door open. Rick looked on with amazement and alarm: the lock had been ruined. He thought it best to say nothing. Annabel hopped in followed by Sam and they drove off, dust swirled behind them.

"I just don't know who that Turk fancied most," said Rick.

"He fancied you!" they blurted out in chorus, and dissolved into giggles.

"You're both drunk."

They continued to giggle.

At midday, they left the road and took a track down to the sea. The trees crowded down to the water's edge. Rick and Annabel went for a swim, walking over the black sand to get to the water. Sam complained of

Road trip Isfahan 1969

stomach cramps and sat on the bank and watched. As usual some boys turned up and joined in the fun. Suddenly their father appeared looking anything but friendly and made it plain that trespassers were not welcome. He was shouting at them and it was clear that the nearly naked female form was causing offence. They fled as fast as they could. The route continued along the rocky coast.

-§-

Trabzon, when they got there, was fascinating. It had a mediaeval feel to it. Rick and Annabel wandered down a street devoted to copper smiths; pots, pans and lamps were piled high outside the shops; men were working away in dark recesses. In the street of the wood carvers they peered into the dim interior of a workshop to see men turning wood on ancient lathes.

"They have been making the legs for tables and chairs like that for at least two thousand years, I should think," said Rick.

"Probably only one thousand years," Annabel corrected him.

Rick wasn't annoyed, he believed everything she told him. In the food market, they bought a huge earthenware pot full of yogurt with a blue bead tied to the handle. After a few days the yogurt began to ferment and had to be thrown away but they kept the jug, as a memento.

"We better get back to the Land Rover and see how Sam is feeling," said Annabel.

Road trip Isfahan 1969

Chapter Eight
Trabzon to Mianduab
Black Sea to the Zagros Mountains

They left the coast on a dirt road, which climbed steeply up the side of the gorge. There was a stream running along the bottom with a rickety footbridge. The mountains on either side were steep bare rock and scree with just the occasional thorn bush. At last the gorge widened out into a valley where there was a village with a petrol station. It was late afternoon; they stopped and asked if they could camp. Leaving the Land Rover beside the garage, they humped their stuff into the field. After the mandatory swim in the river, and hair wash, they wandered back towards the tent. Sam came up behind Rick and grabbed his long, lank but no longer greasy hair.

"You could be mistaken for a girl, your hair's so long!"

"And you're so pretty!" added Annabel taking another handful of mane and giving it a tug, she continued: "We must do something about it; I'm going to give you a haircut. We need you to at least look like a man. It won't do to let people think we are three defenceless girls."

"No, let me!" said Sam.

Rick sat down with his back to her; he was not at all sure what she had in mind but he liked the way she ran her fingers through his hair. Annabel was watching and he hoped she was feeling a little bit jealous. Sam had only just started, when Rick saw out of the corner of his eye a man walking towards them. He took the scissors

Road trip Isfahan 1969

from Sam and started snipping away. The girls tried unsuccessfully to suppress their giggles.

"What's going on?" asked Rick.

Sam regained control enough to open the bottle of Raki and offer a glass to the barber. The four of them sat around talking and drinking. The barber's friend appeared with some hazelnuts, which he offered around. Annabel started to cook the ratatouille, and quite an audience soon surrounded her. As it grew dark more villagers arrived outside the garage and started a traditional Turkish dance.

"Come on," said Sam and boldly joined the dancers who had formed a circle, arms on each other's shoulders.

Annabel and Rick were reluctant but it did not seem to matter that the two girls were the only women there. They circled right, they circled left. They set to the right and set to the left, joined hands and danced into the middle and out again. Then a man took centre stage and danced a jig. Rick kept a very firm arm around Annabel's waist; he was anxious that one of the Turks would lure her away. But he could not keep hold of both girls so he had to let go of Sam. He was not enjoying himself and wondered how he and Annabel could get away and go back to the tent; he wanted to be alone with Annabel, but at the same time felt guilty at the thought of leaving Sam alone with the villagers. The problem was resolved when the headman stopped the dance. The women now appeared and laid out the feast. The men sat down around an enormous silver platter loaded with lamb and rice; while the women sat further back watching the men eating all the best bits. It would be their turn later. Rick and the girls slipped away.

Road trip Isfahan 1969

Annabel and Sam dived into the tent, leaving Rick to keep guard outside. He tried to join them in the tent, wanting to sit and talk, but they shooed him out.

"And don't hang about outside the tent hoping to catch any juicy gossip!" Sam shouted at his retreating back.

Turks came and went, but nobody bothered them.

-§-

After a breakfast of fried eggs, flat bread and tea, they loaded their stuff into the back of Land Rover, filled the water carriers, fuelled up and were off. The road climbed a valley between steep mountains. They passed people hurrying to market. Men drove donkeys heavily laden with mysterious sacks. Women walked behind, their heads and sometimes their faces covered by a black veil. One or two carried enormous black umbrellas to ward off the sun.

They stopped at the market to buy provisions and examine the things on display: pots and rugs seemed to be the most popular items.

"If only there was more room in the Land Rover, I would buy a few carpets and sell them when we get home," said Sam.

"Or keep them. They would go really well in my flat."

"I didn't know you had a flat, Annabel," said Rick.

"I don't right now, but I will someday. I can't live at home for ever."

The road rose steeply to the top of the pass, spectacular views of mountains scorched a sandy brown

Road trip Isfahan 1969

by the relentless sun stretched away into the distance; the descent along a narrow road clinging to the side of the mountain was perilous. It was terribly hot; as soon as they could they stopped again for sips of Canada Dry and a rest.

Sam had become very quiet.

"Are you OK, Sam," asked Rick.

Sam whispered something to Annabel, who was sitting between them.

"What is it?" asked Rick.

"Women's trouble, no business of yours," said Annabel.

The road descended into a wide valley with Erzurum in the centre, the last big town before Persia. They looked about for a campsite and found a very bleak and dusty square of ground by a petrol station outside the city. Some Frenchmen had already pitched their tent. Annabel got into conversation and it turned out they had run into a horse in the night.

"I am not planning to drive at night," said Rick.

Annabel translated for him.

"They want to know how many kilometres we usually do in a day?"

"About three hundred," said Rick.

The conversation continued in French; she turned back to him and said: "They have managed twice that on a good day."

-§-

"I am happy to take it easy today and spend the day looking round Erzurum, Sam," said Rick.

Road trip Isfahan 1969

"No, I'm OK. It's just cramps, let's press on."

"We'll do a quick shop," said Annabel.

Leaving Sam in the Land Rover they explored the narrow alleyways of the old city. In the covered market, carpet sellers were vying for trade. Occasional stalls sold lokum and dates but not the vegetables and oil they needed. They came out in a square on one side of which was a mosque, not the like the opulent Blue Mosque in Istanbul, but made from plain unadorned mud bricks.

A crowd gathered round them. The older men were muttering and gesticulating, the children started to press against them tweaking the hairs on Rick's bare legs and trying to stroke Annabel's long blond hair. A policeman shouldered his way through the crowd waving his baton. He explained in excellent English that the men were offended by Rick's shorts and by Annabel's bare head. They backed hastily away offering humble apologies, avoiding the horse drawn cabs that were plying their trade up and down the main thoroughfare, made it back to the Land Rover and headed out of town.

Rick started to laugh. "I have never had the hairs on my legs pulled like that; I should have known not to wear shorts and you shouldn't go about bare headed, Annabel."

"First you criticise me for wearing a dress and now you want me to wear a burqa! Next you'll demand that I walk behind you like a submissive little wifey."

"I'm just saying that we should respect local customs, wifey!"

Annabel pinched the skin on his forearm and gave it a vicious twist.

Road trip Isfahan 1969

"OK children! Calm down! Sounds like you had a narrow escape there. Let's learn something and dress with more decorum next time."

"More decorum!" they screamed in unison. "You're not our mother!"

They were leaving the mountains behind and driving across a wide plain towards the Persian border. The harvest had been gathered in and on the outskirts of the villages were great piles of grain, being winnowed by men with shovels and pitchforks; teams of oxen driven by small boys were threshing the corn. The land was bare and arid. In the distance was the snow covered peak of Mount Ararat. Annabel photographed the mountain and Rick photographed her taking the picture.

"You're wasting precious film, Rick."

"It's the only picture that I will really treasure. I'll have it framed and keep it on my desk."

"Men really do that, Annabel," Sam warned her. "The wife and then children when they come along!"

"That's why he is wasting film, Sam. I'm never going to let Rick get that close to me!"

He smiled but kept his mouth shut.

Another 200 miles and they arrived at the border, the Turkish officials waved them through but on the Persian side there were forms to fill in and 100 rials[2] to pay. The girls thought the Persian officer rather attractive in his smart uniform. He had a ready laugh and advised them: "When in Persia, keep smiling".

Back on tarmac'd roads they did 50 miles in an hour and stopped at a chai house. It was the usual sparsely furnished room with a mud floor, and a samovar in one corner; a flickering flame kept the tea hot. Annabel and

Road trip Isfahan 1969

Sam got into conversation with some students: a Dutch hitch-hiker and two Germans who were on their way home after a cycling tour of Persia. The patron brought over small glasses of tea, with a sugar lump, hacked off a sugar loaf, in the saucer. The truck drivers poured their tea into the saucer and let the sugar dissolve before sipping it.

"I've never seen an actual sugar loaf before," said Rick.

Annabel smiled and raised her saucer to her lips like she did this sort of thing every day.

"Where have you been staying?" she asked the German girl.

"Oh it's not safe to sleep here or in any of the road side hostelries, in Persia."

"We always find a place well off the road and away from the villages," added her companion. "There is a bridge over a dry river bed not far down the road, where we spent last night."

"I was going to ask the owner if we could camp behind the house," said Rick.

"No, I really would not do that," said the Dutchman. "Although I have always found the Persians very friendly and hospitable, I prefer to sleep in the countryside. I will show you the place by the bridge, if you like."

The German cyclists waved goodbye and the four explorers headed away from the village, towards the bridge.

"I don't really like the look of this place. There is too much going on," said Rick.

Road trip Isfahan 1969

"It'll be fine," said the Dutchman. "I was here last night and I know the night watchman."

"That's reassuring, Hedda," said Sam.

"It's too late to look for another place now," said Annabel.

The workmen left and the night watchman came over and greeted them. He recognised Hedda. Annabel cooked up some vegetables in soup and handed it round with bread. Hedda turned out to be an engineer; he was hitch hiking up from Kuwait, where he had been involved in drilling for oil. The girls slept in the tent, Rick on his camp-bed and Hedda on the ground.

The night passed quietly enough until some workmen arrived.

"Rick!" Annabel called out. "What is going on?"

Rick put his head into the tent.

"Just some blokes. Our friend, the night watchman is sorting them out."

The girls looked anxiously up at him.

"I do hope it's going to be alright," said Annabel.

"You'll be fine," said Rick and went back to his sleeping bag.

"I think the night watchman must have said something about us," said Rick.

"Yes, he will make sure we are not disturbed," agreed Hedda.

-§-

The rising sun soon made the tent too hot for comfort. The girls appeared and Rick handed out cups of tea.

Road trip Isfahan 1969

Annabel stared blearily at him and stretched out a lazy hand to ruffle his shorn locks: "So beautiful!" she said.

They left the Dutch student on the bridge and headed for Tabriz. Rick had dreadful stomach ache, which was shortly followed by a brief but violent bout of Delhi belly. Sam was very concerned.

"I just over indulged in soup and watermelon last night," said Rick.

The road was fast and smooth compared to the roads between Trabzon and Erzurum, and they were soon in Tabriz: a modern concrete jungle. It was Friday, the day of rest in a Muslim country, so all the banks were shut, however in a travel agency they changed some American dollars.

"Next stop Kermanshah."

The road soon deteriorated into a dirt track; the surface corrugations made the Land Rover vibrate alarmingly. The southerly wind was scorching and there was no shade. In the distance the camels and tents of the Kurds could be seen across the flat and arid plane. They passed a huge salt lake.

"Stop the bus!" said Annabel. "I can't read the map with everything shaking like this."

Rick pulled up beside a village store and went off to buy Canada Dry, bread and goat's cheese. When he came back the three of them studied the map. The village was called Mianduab. It looked as if they should take the right-hand fork out of the village, if they wanted to keep to the main road.

"Off we go again," said Annabel with great confidence.

Road trip Isfahan 1969

As darkness fell, they came upon an army post: a small garrison, guarding the frontier with Iraq. Rick was not at all sure how the soldiers would react to a man and two young women appearing in their territory. They might well regard them as intruders and arrest them. Any anxiety was quickly dispelled. The soldiers turned out to be most hospitable and welcomed the strangers; they brought bread and cheese and herbs to the tent and would not hear of payment. The sergeant who spoke good English stayed and chatted. Rick introduced the girls: "This is my wife," indicating Annabel. "And this is her servant," indicating Sam.

The sergeant could not help laughing: "I am sure you students are too poor to get married let alone employ servants!"

He went off to his quarters laughing. He had obviously worked out that they were part of the huge exodus from Europe making for Katmandu and beyond; a migration that the law enforcement agencies in Turkey, Persia and even Afghanistan must have become accustomed to in the 1960s.

Annabel was not disguised as a Muslim wife and did not behave like one. She was very modestly dressed in a very long blue cotton nightdress that buttoned up to the throat; a white lace collar topped off the ensemble. Sam on the other hand was most daringly attired in blue shorts, a white open necked shirt, and tennis shoes. If the sergeant found her attire shocking, he was too polite and urbane to say so.

"It's your night off Annabel, we'll do the cooking," said Rick.

Road trip Isfahan 1969

Annabel looked at him suspiciously.
"Can I trust you?"
"With your life. I won't let you down."
He made an omelette, while Sam cut up the bread and cheese that the soldiers had supplied.

Road trip Isfahan 1969

Chapter Nine
Mianduab to Baba Jan

The soldiers were up early, and Rick went with them to fill the water carriers. The soldiers had great barrels to replenish. Rick left Annabel and Sam in their sleeping bags and drove to a village up in the hills, where the women, dressed in long black gowns decorated with coins, were filling their pots at a well. When the women saw the soldiers approaching, they moved aside and let the men fill their water carriers, watching in complete silence. Back at the outpost Rick asked a soldier for hot water for shaving and the man brought eau-de-cologne as well. Rick dabbed it on a cut saying to Sam:

"Prevents infection, you know and I am sure you won't mind the smell."

"Makes a change."

Annabel emerged from the tent and looked around myopically. She had given up on contact lenses because in the heat and the dust they made her eyes sore and without her glasses she could hardly see a thing.

"You look just like Moly," said Rick, thinking of Wind in the Willows.

Annabel screwed up her eyes: "Is that you, Rat, smelling like a tart?"

"But much prettier," he added.

"Too late, Rick," warned Sam.

"I'm a fat black blind burrowing creature, am I?"

Annabel slapped him around the head so hard that he was knocked sideways.

Road trip Isfahan 1969

"No, no, really I love your big blue eyes and I love the way you look, not anything like a mole," he pleaded in vain.

"Sorry, matey you've just blown it. No excuses; now I know what you really feel about me."

They were interrupted by the sergeant inviting them to breakfast on the roof of the mess. Tea was served in the usual little glass cups on a saucer accompanied by bread and yogurt. When they asked the way to Kermanshah they were told they were on the border with Iraq. The Sergeant told them to return to Mianduab and turn right. They packed up and left after exchanging farewells and photos. The sergeant wrote out his home address in Arabic script.

They regained the road to Kermanshah after about half an hour and soon found a river well away from habitation. Rick watched as Annabel and Sam swam upstream with lazy strokes. Naked, they looked like water nymphs out of a Victorian illustration. He plunged in and swam after them.

"Go and get my towel, Rick," said Annabel.

"And mine," Sam called after him.

He got out, pulled on his shorts and returned to the river bank.

"Here you are."

"Look away, Rick," said Annabel.

Sam was not so bashful; she strode up to him and grabbed her towel. Annabel decorously wrapped hers around her slight figure and tilted her head, wringing the water out of her long hair. She squinted up at him as if aware of what was going through his mind.

"Penny for your thoughts, Rick."

Road trip Isfahan 1969

He blew her a kiss.

He turned and walked back to the Land Rover, what a girl!

The day was hotter than ever and the road rose steeply into the Zagros Mountains. At one point it was so hot and the road so steep that the Land Rover boiled and they had to stop and let it cool down. After a while Rick gingerly unscrewed the radiator cap and poured in some of the precious drinking water.

"Is the engine alright?" asked Sam.

"I think it will be fine now," answered Rick. "Anyway we will soon know if it isn't."

On they went over very bumpy dirt roads, as they hit one pothole there was crash from the back, where the yogurt pot was stored.

"Watch what you're doing; slow down!" the girls shouted.

They stopped and got out to investigate. The pot was smashed in two halves. Annabel put an arm around Rick's shoulders.

"Never mind, I'm sure you will be able to mend it. It wasn't your fault."

He tried to put his arm around her waist but she skipped away.

In places the road was properly tarmac'd and they could speed up then suddenly the tarmac would end in a small precipice. It was not good for the nerves. There was nowhere suitable to stop for the night until eventually they came to a field, but a light moving about in the distance spooked the girls. They drove on again until after dark, exhausted they pulled off the road. The girls slept in the Land Rover and Rick put up his camp-

Road trip Isfahan 1969

bed alongside. They were too tired to eat, or even talk. It was hot and uncomfortable; no one got much sleep until dawn when a cool breeze sprang up. Rick was keen to get on and as it became light, he started to pack up. Annabel was not happy at being disturbed and told him to shove off in no uncertain terms. Both girls started shouting:

"Where is the chai?"

"No chai here. Chai in Kermanshah."

Half an hour later they arrived in the town. They need to re-fuel, but had no Persian money. To Rick's surprise the garage accepted American dollars, and gave them rials in change, just about enough for three cups of tea. The chai man wanted more but Annabel charmed him into accepting what they had.

"You could haggle the hind legs off a donkey."

She ignored him.

They sat and watched the world go by: black robed women were busy shopping while the chai shop filled up with men who, it seemed were looking forward to sitting there all day exchanging news and playing backgammon. Towards midday, the bank opened, they changed travellers' cheques and asked the cashier the way to Khorramabad. The man had no idea and strangely nobody else they asked in the town seemed to have heard of Khorramabad no matter how Rick pronounced it. For once even Annabel was unable to make herself understood. Bartholomew's map of the Middle East was the only chart they had.

"What's the scale?" asked Annabel. "There isn't much detail, and it certainly doesn't show Nurabad or Baba Jan. We need a small scale local map."

Road trip Isfahan 1969

"One inch is sixty miles," said Rick. "I'm sure Bab Jan is just round the corner. Didn't Prof. Goodchild send you a map or instructions of some sort, Sam?"

"Yes but Jon (the bastard) took it with him. From what I can remember, if we get to Nurabad, which is half way between Kermanshah and Khorramabad then Baba Jan is just 4km to the West."

"Great!"

They set off again. Annabel was singing to herself.

"What is that tune, Annabel?" Rick asked her.

"Gilbert and Sullivan," she replied.

"Three little girls from school are we," she sang and Sam joined in.

Late in the afternoon they arrived in Khorramabad, and stopped for chai and a kebab. At last, after asking half a dozen people they found someone from Nurabad. In a mixture of Farsi and halting English, the man explained that they had come down the wrong road. He could not say how far it was to Nurabad but he estimated one farsank, which is as far as a man and his donkey can walk in a day.

They set off again up a dirt road full of huge potholes. It wound uphill into the mountains, hairpin bend after hairpin bend. Suddenly the Land Rover slewed across the road and came to a halt. Annabel clutched Rick's arm:

"What's happened?"

Rick got out of the Land Rover. There was a four-inch nail in the left front tyre, completely puncturing it. Annabel climbed down and helped Rick to change the wheel. He watched her as she replaced the wheel nuts, the look of concentration on her face made him smile.

Road trip Isfahan 1969

"Here, let me."

There was brief scuffle for the wheel brace which involved more physical contact than was really necessary. Annabel won, and for a moment leant against him. He could feel her breath on his chest. Sam sat at the side of the track and continued to read her book, ignoring them.

At last, after about 30km they arrived in Nurabad. It was growing dark. They stopped in yet another chai house to ask for Baba Jan; all they got were blank stares. Rick's earlier optimism evaporated, he felt grubby, tired and anxious.

"I really do not want to spend another night out in the open when we're so close," he said.

"When in doubt ask a Policeman, as your mother would say," muttered Sam.

At that very moment a policeman turned up; even more surprising was that he knew Professor Goodchild and was on his way to visit her. They offered to give him a lift as, rather strangely, he did not seem to have any means of transport. They started off up a very narrow track, forded a muddy stream, drove through a village, crossed a crumbling stone bridge, jolted over a ditch and were at last in the village of Baba Jan. They pulled up outside a large square one storey stone building with a flat roof, which turned out to be the cookhouse and mess. The Prof was out; she had gone down to Kermanshah to get her Land Rover fixed. None of those left behind seemed to be expecting them. Then an American student appeared out of the darkness.

"Hi. I'm Martha and you must be the students Prof has been expecting. How was the journey out?"

Road trip Isfahan 1969

Without waiting for a reply, she led them into the mess and introduced Hassan: cook and general factotum. They sat down around a huge deal table and stared about them almost in a state of shock.

"We've arrived in Baba Jan! I can't quite believe it!" said Rick.

"I can. I never doubted that we would get here, even for a minute," said Annabel loyally.

She patted him like he was her favourite dog. Sam just snorted and laid her head on her outstretched arms and fell asleep.

The room was vast and bare. The crudely rendered stone walls and timbered ceiling made the place feel like an old barn. This impression was enhanced by pungent animal smells related to cooking on dung. It was hard to see anything at all in the dim light of the candles. Hassan handed round great mugs of milky tea, English style, and then heated up rice and chicken, the remains of the evening meal.

Martha showed them to their quarters: a house in its own walled courtyard. They had the whole place to themselves. The girls took their suitcases, rucksacks and camp-beds out of the back of the Land Rover, started to unpack and got ready for bed. But Rick had to take the policeman home. Martha came along to keep him company and to show him the way back. They deposited the policeman at the police house in Nurabad and headed for Baba Jan. Martha was a good listener and Rick gave her a brief resume of their journey out. Martha filled him in on life in camp. There were seven people who had been there since the beginning of August. Professor

Road trip Isfahan 1969

Susan Goodchild was in charge. Martha described her as tall and thin with short grey hair, en brosse.

"Academic and quiet but with a dry sense of humour. Then there is Charles, also from Oxford, he is writing a PhD. Prof lets him organise the day to day work of the dig and oversee the other students."

She did not seem to like Charles; she found him a bit stuck up.

"I guess it's just that I can't relate to the English gent in him."

"Annabel thinks the world of him," Rick said. "But he and I did not get on well at school. I remember him as bit of a bully. I haven't seen him since he went up to Oxford."

"Sounds like you will be competing for Annabel's attention."

"No, not at all!"

Back at the house, Rick tiptoed into the bedroom and fell over a half-unpacked suitcase.

"What the hell?" from Sam.

"Help! Help! I'm being attacked!" from Annabel

"Fuck off Rick, don't go assaulting Annabel at this time of night.

"Oh it's you Rick. That's alright then."

Rick found his camp-bed and sleeping bag.

"Calm down little tigers!"

But they were asleep. He crept out onto the roof, which turned out to be the best place to be; it was cool and relatively free from bedbugs.

Chapter Ten
Baba Jan

That first morning Rick lay on his camp-bed on the roof of the house and watched the sun rise in splendour over the mountaintops: saffron at first then red and gold reflected off the high clouds. He thought a while about the journey out. It was hard to believe that they had made it, his mind drifted towards the girls. They had been amazing. If Jon had come, he might have been a great help, except that he was a useless driver, he would have argued about the route with Annabel and had deeply offended Sam. In the event, they had coped without him and the girls had remained cool in situations that might have caused alarm in anyone less stout-hearted. He respected Annabel more than ever and now that they had got over their initial difficulties, he felt they had developed a real friendship.

He got up and stretched; before him was the village, consisting of about a dozen or more small square single-storey houses built of stone, each standing in its own large courtyard, surrounded by high walls. The people had moved out of their dwellings and lived in the large black tents beyond the threshing floor. He could see them now, way below him, men and women, winnowing the corn, using pitchforks and wooden shovels. Beyond the tents were herds of black long haired goats, and beyond that the peaks of the Zagros mountains. To the north was the huge mound or tepi where the excavation was going on. He felt that he was on top of the world.

Road trip Isfahan 1969

There was a scream from the room below. Sam was shouting something and Annabel was groaning and blaspheming at the same time. He hurried to see what was going on.

"Oh and the smell is awful; I can't go there and I'm bursting, what shall I do Sam?"

"Hold on, Annabel," said Sam, "Rick will think of something."

"Why me?"

"Because 1. You're practical. 2. You're a man. 3. You love lavatory jokes. I can tell you - even your sense of humour is going to be strained by the bog here," said Sam.

"Where is the bog?" asked Rick.

"In there!" they yelled, pointing to a small dark recess.

He went in and looked around. The smell was truly awful. The girls were right about that. In the dim light, he could see that a trench had been dug in the floor and it extended through the wall so that any liquid content could flow out of the house and down the cliff towards the stream.

"Sorry about this, girls, but you will just have to use a bucket until I unblock the loo."

There were plenty of buckets in the courtyard; he fetched one, then took two others down to the stream. It was hard work carrying two full pails the seventy yards back up the steep hill to the house. After more than a dozen trips, the trench was well flushed and the flies and the stench had almost gone. A final trip to the stream to wash and he was ready for breakfast.

Road trip Isfahan 1969

He joined the girls and the others around the table. Hassan fried bread in sugar and lemon juice, served up with scrambled eggs and English breakfast tea, it was delicious. Sam was wriggling about and scratching her stomach. He sat down beside her.

"What's up Sam?"

She pulled up her shirt so that he could see a ring of red bites around her waist. Barry introduced himself as another student and peered over the table to get a good look at Sam's middle. She covered herself and gave him a hard stare.

"Bedbugs," said Barry. "I didn't mean to pry, but we have all suffered. Hassan has some spray that will help."

"Anthisan cream will help the itching, I've got some back at the house," said Rick.

"Why hasn't Annabel been bitten?" Sam asked, frowning.

"Because she doesn't wear pyjamas, the beg bugs seem to like to burrow around the waist band so you are better off wearing a nightie. Also, it is a fact that bedbugs have preferences, depending on all sorts of things," said Rick.

"Like how sweet you are," said Annabel.

"Then they should be biting you and not me; don't you agree Rick?" said Sam.

"How can I say when I have never tasted either of you?"

-§-

The students trouped off towards the tepi, Sam and Annabel went with them, Rick watched as they climbed

Road trip Isfahan 1969

the steep mound to start the day's work. There was not much actual digging to do because the men from the village were employed to do that. The students spent their time scraping away at things with a trowel or drawing artefacts such as earthenware pots, or tiny pieces of Bronze Age jewellery.

Rick went to help Hassan with the domestic side of the camp. This morning he wanted to be driven into Nurabad to buy food, candles and shovels for the dig. Hassan did not haggle over these day-to-day items; Rick had thought that people in the Middle East haggled over everything. Just as they were getting ready to return one of the villagers turned up and asked to be driven to see a relative. It wasn't far out of their way and Hassan obviously gained kudos by having a vehicle and a driver at his disposal. They were back by midday.

While Hassan was preparing lunch, Rick went up onto the tepi to see how things were going. Sam was overseeing a work party, and Annabel was helping with the scale drawings; just as he arrived they unearthed a bronze belt buckle. They were kneeling in the dirt, stroking the earth off the buckle with a paintbrush.

"Wow! Take a photo while it is in situ, we'll clean it up this evening, then you can draw it," said Sam.

Annabel was in charge of the dig's camera. They were both so engrossed in their find that they did not notice Rick peering over their shoulders.

"Where have you sprung from?" asked Annabel as she stood up.

"I went to Nurabad with Hassan. Do you want lunch yet? Hassan is getting it ready."

Road trip Isfahan 1969

The days passed, they each had their routine; Rick got to know Hassan quite well. As they drove backwards and forwards to Nurabad, Hassan would gossip about what was going on in the village. It was not always the peaceful scene it appeared. Brothers got into a fight and one cut off the other's ear. On another occasion, there was a murder: a blow from a rock killed the victim. The murderer was caught but he was not handed over to the police. The village elders sorted it out. The family of the murderer was ordered to pay the victim's family blood money, which in this case meant several sheep and goats. All this in pidgin English, which meant each story took hours.

Hassan began to trust Rick and sent him into Nurabad to buy bread, meat and vegetables on his own. Schooled by Hassan and armed with a Persian phrase book, he entered the shop.

"Salam alekum" he greeted the butcher. "Shak hadi?"

The man looked puzzled for a moment, then disappeared into the back of the shop chuckling to himself. He reappeared with a kilo of mince.

"Khely mamnoon," Rick thanked the man, wondering what was making him laugh.

Later, when he asked Prof she explained to him that he had asked the butcher to "Chop up the cow."

-§-

Gradually Rick and the girls got to know the others: Martha was from Maine, she was the friendliest, the others were Sasha (a man's name in Hungary), Barry

Road trip Isfahan 1969

from Birmingham, Nigel from Nottingham and Ben from Boston.

Friday was a day of rest for the archaeologists, arranged by Prof to fit in with the villagers' week. She suggested they go for a ride, as a diversion from the serious work of digging. Rick and the girls joined the others on an expedition that would have done credit to the Wild West. Hassan had been talking to the headman of the village who said he could provide half a dozen horses. The horses came saddled and bridled with tack that resembled nothing Rick had ever seen, not even in cowboy films. The saddles were wooden, covered with smelly rags, and the bridles were very primitive indeed. The reins and the head band were made of plaited cloth. Some of the undergraduates had little experience of horses and they could not control the beasts very well. Sam, however was in her element.

"Talk to your pony," she told Barry.

"What shall I say?" he asked.

"Go whoa, and shush, shush. Ponies like that," she advised.

It soon became obvious that Prof had done this before and her nag set off at a sedate pace, but Martha's horse wanted to get in front and barged past Sam's horse, which then started trotting to keep up.

"Whoa, whoa!" crooned Sam and brought her pony back to a walk.

Barry was not used to riding and was hardly able to hold on. Sasha, true to his Hungarian roots proved a very dashing horseman, and was soon cantering on in front. Rick was at ease on his mount and was just admiring

Road trip Isfahan 1969

Annabel's seat, when his steed stumbled and pitched him off over its ears, into a prickly bush.

"That hasn't happened to me in a long time," he said looking suitably embarrassed, while trying to pick thorns out of his arms.

Annabel reined in her pony and tried to look concerned. But when she saw that the thorns weren't only in his arms she dismounted and giggling, started to try to get them out of his backside. Prof stopped and held the horses while they sorted themselves out.

"Drop your pants!" she ordered. "Annabel can't get the thorns out of your arse until you do."

Annabel lost control and was helpless with laughter.

"Pull yourself together girl. I am not going to wait around all day."

Annabel got herself under control and picked the largest thorns out of her friend's bare bottom.

"Careful! That's bloody painful," he warned her.

She gave him a sharp slap.

"Pull your pants up and let's go!" she said.

Rick shortened his stirrups and cautiously mounted. With his knees on the pommel he looked like a jockey riding along with his bum in the air.

After about an hour they turned for home. At first they ambled along but as anyone who has ever had anything to do with horses will know, they go much faster if they think they are going back to their stables. The last furlong became a headlong gallop. Sam's years at the Pony Club had not been wasted after all. Poor Barry and Nigel did not have the same advantage; they soon fell off and their nags galloped home without them. Prof kept her horse under control, so it became a wild

Road trip Isfahan 1969

race between Rick (standing in the stirrups), Annabel, Martha, Sasha and Sam who won by a neck. Sasha was most put out and tried to pretend he had pulled up to spare his horse.

"But in Hungary we ride the horses so hard that sometimes they drop dead under us."

"And what about the women?" gasped Barry as he caught up.

"Oh yes, them too."

Prof pretended not to hear, but Martha and Sam laughed out loud. Annabel doesn't like smut, thought Rick and looked at her to see her reaction: she was grinning. Back at base, they loosened the horses' girths and took them down to the stream to let them drink, then back to the black tents.

Hot and smelling of horse they went off to the hammam in Nurabad. The baths, with separate rooms for men and women, had showers, steam rooms, freezing cold plunge pools, and cubicles for a massage. Rick was uncomfortable sitting in the steam room, his bum was stinging; plunging into a cold bath did bring some relief. The massage was very relaxing and he found himself wondering what it would be like if he could persuade Annabel to give him a massage.

The group wandered through the market place to a tea shop. The towns people had grown accustomed to seeing the students and were not offended by men in shorts or women who did not cover their heads and even showed their legs.

"They just think you're tarts," Rick told the girls.

Road trip Isfahan 1969

They did not bother to reply to this insult but beat him mercilessly on his sore bottom with their riding whips.

"You should have given those whips back to Hassan," said Rick, with feeling.

"I love people watching," said Sam "Just look at the different garments."

The local women wore cotton dresses with a floral print and over this a highly decorated waistcoat covered with silver coins. Their long black hair was tied back with a bandana. The young girls were dressed in similar very long cotton print dresses, but with no waistcoat. The boys wore check trousers and boots like their fathers with a long shirt hanging to their knees.

"Charles II started the craze for wearing Persian waistcoats."

"How do you know that, Sam?" asked Annabel.

"My first degree was in the history of fashion. Being fashionable was everything at the court of Charles II, and indeed in France."

Rick was too sore to bother to listen to what the girls were saying; he was wishing he had kept his mouth shut. Girls don't like being teased he reflected.

-§-

"Party time!" announced Martha.

"What's the occasion?" asked Rick.

"We don't need an excuse to party, but it just happens that Barry is leaving tomorrow."

Road trip Isfahan 1969

Rick went off to tell the girls: "Um… I wonder if you could help me get the rest of the thorns out of my bottom, before we go to the party?"

He looked at Annabel who looked at Sam.

"I will if Sam will help me; safety in numbers, eh Sam?" she said with a grin.

They moved a bed near the window to where the afternoon light was streaming in. Sam got the tweezers that she used for plucking her eyebrows and Rick lay prone on the bed. He was already sweating in anticipation of what was to come. Annabel held the bottle of TCP and balls of cotton wool.

"Loosen your belt," commanded Sam.

Rick complied and the girls grabbed his shorts and pulled them down, together with his pants. They smiled at each other and set to work. Sam gripped each thorn with the tweezers and Annabel dabbed the antiseptic onto the puncture wound. Rick writhed in agony and bit his knuckles. The girls worked away like professionals until they were satisfied that all the foreign bodies had been removed and the chances of infection killing their patient reduced. They stood back and admired their work:

"What a beautiful behind!" exclaimed Sam.

"It would be if it was not covered in red blotches!" said Annabel and gave it a smack.

"Ow! Leave me alone!"

He pulled up his pants and tried to stand but came over faint and quickly sat down again.

Annabel put her arms around him. She peered into his face:

"You're not crying, are you?"

Road trip Isfahan 1969

She rocked him from side to side. Rick relaxed, this was more than adequate compensation for a painful and even humiliating experience. He felt grateful, even (surprising in the circumstances) lustful. But there was no time to dally. The party was already in full swing when the three of them got back to the main hall.

Martha was in charge and she had mixed up a powerful rum punch from a concoction of dubious local spirits and fruit juice, sweetened enough to disguise its potency. She had also acquired a sound system from somewhere and the Rolling Stones were blaring out of the speakers. Rick could not dance with both girls at once and he thought it would be rude to leave Sam out so he asked her first and they bopped away bouncing off and bumping into vaguely recognised shapes. It was hard to see who was who in the gloom. They took a break from dancing and Rick went to get more punch. When he returned, Sam was gone. He looked around; she was on the other side of the room talking to Barry. Feeling hot and in need of fresh air he went outside and took the stairs up onto the roof.

The night was cool and he thought he was on his own. Without street lights, the stars seemed brighter than he had ever seen them. He took a deep breath and gazed upwards. Then in a corner he noticed Annabel; she was kissing Charles, it could not be anyone else, even though it was hard to see anything definite by the light of the crescent moon. He was just about to go over to them and confront Annabel with her treachery when Sam came up behind him and put her arms around his waist. She gave him a gentle squeeze and standing on tip toe whispered in his ear:

Road trip Isfahan 1969

"Leave them alone. There is something I want to show you."

Curiosity won over jealousy; they left the roof and wandered towards the stream. Sam stopped beneath a tree and put her arms around his neck. She kissed him on the lips. He was taken aback by her sudden move and murmured something about Annabel, Sam kissed him harder. Coming up for air she said:

"Forget Annabel, just for one night. I am going to teach you a something that you will never forget."

She started kissing him again and with even more passion. He surrendered and did his best to push his tongue down her throat, but she slipped out of his arms and sank to her knees. He felt her undo his belt:

"Stand still, PP!"

"Stop, Sam stop, or............"

He never did get to finish the sentence. They wandered back to the party, holding hands.

"Sam......"

"Yes PP?"

"Sam. What does PP stand for?"

She burst out laughing:

"Priapic Prince. It is what I used to call my pony, just to shock the gymkhana brigade. By the way: your flies are undone."

As they approached the main hall, they met Annabel and Charles, his arm was around her waist.

Rick's elation subsided and he began to feel stupid and inadequate. The girls were running rings around him and he was about as much use as a bear in a pit. He went off to bed feeling confused and angry; not at all able to understand his feelings. He lay awake waiting for the

Road trip Isfahan 1969

girls to come back to the house. It seemed like hours before he heard them singing and giggling as they blundered about trying to find their beds in the room below

Road trip Isfahan 1969

Chapter Eleven
Annabel Gets a Fever

Rick climbed the side of the tepi looking for Annabel and Sam. He wondered how they would greet him after last night. He had deliberately avoided joining them at breakfast. He suspected they might be feeling a bit sheepish. He certainly was. When he did catch sight of Annabel his misgivings vanished. She looked pale under her tan, she was clearly ill.

"Oh Rick, I'm not feeling at all well."

"What's wrong?"

"I've a splitting headache."

He felt her forehead with the back of his hand. She was burning hot. He took her temperature and it was raised. The Prof wandered over.

"It's just a bad hangover, people underestimate the effect of alcohol in this heat," she said.

"I expect you're dehydrated," said Rick. "Come back to the house and I'll bring water and two Aspirin."

"Yes, I'll lie down for a bit."

She tottered down the tepi; Rick realised she wasn't going to make it back the house.

"Sit on my shoulders and I'll carry you up the hill."

They went swaying up the hill. He fetched some water from the kitchen that had been boiled and cooled. Hassan was responsible for the drinking water, but this time Rick saw to it himself. He gave her aspirin and paracetamol and she slept most of the day.

"Would you like some supper?"

"No thanks, Rick, I'm feeling a bit sick and my headache isn't getting any better."

Road trip Isfahan 1969

He dosed her up and she went back to sleep. Sam joined them.

"What do you think it is?" she asked.

"Some sort of tummy bug. The sanitation around here is a bit primitive."

He turned to Annabel: "You're drinking OK so things should improve in 24/48 hours."

But next day it was clear that something was seriously wrong. Her headache was worse and her temperature was now higher. Sam and Rick went to see Prof. They found her up on the tepi directing operations but she dropped what she was doing and came back to the house to assess Annabel for herself. She looked grave.

"The nearest telephone is in Nurabad. I'll drive down to there now and telephone Mr Jasseri."

"Who is Mr Jasseri?" asked Sam.

"He is an old friend. It's through him I got invited to excavate the tepi here. His place is large, luxurious and has all the mod-cons. It is much more civilised; Annabel can rest up and get well again there. Also, he has access to the best doctors. Last year when one of the undergraduates had a bad accident Mr J sorted him out. He would not hear of us paying the surgeon."

"That sounds good," said Rick. "I don't think Annabel will be very comfortable here."

"Even quite minor infections can turn nasty in this climate. I know Mr J will want her to stay with him. So, don't hang about, get going now."

"Thank you so much," said Sam and gave the professor a hug.

Road trip Isfahan 1969

"Take Hassan with you; he'll show you the way." Prof shouted over her shoulder as she hurried off.

Rick carried Annabel down the hill from the house and laid her in the back of the Land Rover on as many rugs and cushions as he could find. Sam climbed in the back with Annabel, and they were off, jolting over the dirt roads.

"Slow down, Rick. The bumping is making Annabel's headache worse," Sam had to shout to make herself heard above the noise.

Annabel was crying in pain. They crawled along making agonisingly slow progress. Sam kept making reassuring noises; Rick was silent, chewing his lip and blaming himself for not realising sooner how ill Annabel was. It was certainly more serious than a tummy bug; it might be anything from appendicitis to meningitis.

At last they arrived at Mr. Jasseri's house. He was expecting them; the servants had prepared a bed for the patient in a room next to a modern bathroom. There were rugs on the floor but no pictures on the walls and the only windows were high up, overlooking the central courtyard. Rick lifted Annabel up in his arms and she clung to his neck as he carried her into the house and laid her down on a mattress on the floor.

"Thank you," she whispered.

"You will be quite safe here. You'll soon be better."

He kissed her forehead. Meanwhile Hassan was describing the symptoms to Mr. Jasseri who thought she should see his physician.

"Don't waste time. You should go right away," he said to Rick.

Road trip Isfahan 1969

Sam stayed with Annabel, while Rick set off with Hassan to get the doctor.

The doctor grabbed his bag and came with them at once.

Rick watched him examining Annabel.

"You don't mind me staying do you?" he asked.

"No Rick, I want you here," Annabel mumbled.

Rick held her hand. The doctor knelt beside her and examined her abdomen: it was vaguely tender all over, and covered with small rose coloured spots. She had no neck stiffness. He stood up and turned to Rick.

"Mr Jasseri tells me you are a medical student. So, I imagine you will have made the diagnosis."

"The salmon pink spots make me think of Typhoid fever," said Rick.

"Right first time. I will give you a prescription for chloramphenicol to be taken four times a day and morphine for relief of pain."

The physician wrote out a prescription for the course of antibiotics and the strong analgesic, which he handed to Hassan, all the time speaking rapidly in Farsi. It was not at all encouraging that he looked so worried. Rick could not read the prescription which was written in beautiful Arabic script, but he trusted the man.

"Will you stay with Annabel," he asked Sam.

She nodded, and walked with them towards the Land Rover.

"Is Typhoid fever serious, Rick?"

"Once the antibiotics have started to work she will be fine!"

Road trip Isfahan 1969

He tried to sound reassuring, but he could see that Sam was not convinced.

Rick and Hassan took the doctor home and went to get the prescription.

Mr Jasseri was waiting for them when they got back. In response to Rick's questions he explained that the water from the tap in the bathroom was safe to drink and gave orders for a glass and carafe to be fetched from the kitchen. Rick helped Annabel to sit up so that she could sip some water and swallow down the pills. The morphine was in liquid form; she took a swig straight from the bottle.

"Oh Rick, I feel so ill, I ache all over and my head feels as if it is going to explode. Don't leave me."

"You'll be OK. The morphine will soon start to work and then you'll feel much better."

But no sooner were the words out of his mouth than poor Annabel clutched her stomach and tried to get up. Rick helped her to the bathroom and held her head while she vomited in the sink.

"Get out of here!" she warned as she made for the lavatory.

He retreated, until she called him back. The smell was impressive and he was close to retching.

"I'm so sorry Rick, please help me shower." She was near to tears, exhausted.

Rick called Sam for help and between them they undressed Annabel and she sat under the shower, like a small child, the water pouring over her. Sam gently rubbed her dry and Rick carried her back to bed.

"I'm glad you're here Rick, I can't cope with vomit," said Sam.

Road trip Isfahan 1969

Rick smiled and knelt by the bed.

"Now, Sugar, you'll have to try to keep these medicines down this time."

He dosed her all over again and this time she wasn't sick, to his relief.

"Did you call me Sugar?" she managed a weak smile.

Rick sat with her until the morphine took effect and she managed to doze. A servant put his head round the door and said that Mr Jasseri hoped Sam and Rick would join him for supper.

"I have asked my wife to sit with Annabel while we eat," said Mr Jasseri.

"Thank you, that is most kind," said Rick.

A woman wearing the full burqa silently passed them and went into the bedroom, she was followed by her servant carrying fresh sheets and towels.

The women stayed in a separate building and Rick hardly ever saw them and never without a veil. Rick now learned that Hassan normally cooked for Mr Jasseri but he had agreed to help at Baba Jan.

They sat around the low table on cushions. Supper was served on a huge silver dish: it was a delicious meal of stewed chicken and aubergine, on a mound of rice, washed down with whisky and water. But Rick was distracted by thoughts of Annabel. It was hard to sit there and enjoy the feast when she was so ill and unable to join in. Sam did her best to keep the conversation going, and it seemed to Rick that Mr J enjoyed talking to her and was not at all put off by the fact that she was a woman and not wearing a veil.

Road trip Isfahan 1969

When he got back to the sick room Annabel was asleep. The women had arranged a mattress in a corner of the room. He undressed down to his underpants and pulled the quilt up to his chin. Annabel woke several times in the night and he went over to her and supported her in his arms as he coaxed her to take sips of water. He poured another dose of morphine onto a spoon and she swallowed it like an infant. Her fever seemed higher than ever; he fetched a cold wet flannel and gently bathed her face and neck. She rested her head in his lap; it soothed them both, the slow repetitive movement of the cloth over her skin. He began to nod off.

"There there," he murmured, "you'll soon be better."

He believed what he was saying; anything else was unthinkable.

In the morning, her temperature seemed to settle.

"How are you feeling, Sugar?"

She smiled bravely: "Bit better."

"Could you take some soup?"

She nodded uncertainly.

Hassan and Sam took the bus back to the dig. Sam was reluctant to leave, but Annabel seemed to be on the mend and she did not want to let Professor Goodchild down.

The day passed slowly. Rick read to Annabel when she was awake and when she slept he wandered out into the streets to get some air. The servants supplied him with a kebab for lunch which he took on his own. When he got back to the room Annabel was awake, very hot and sweating profusely. He took her temperature: it was up again. She looked grey and ill; she could not get comfortable. He helped her to take more morphine and

Road trip Isfahan 1969

added two paracetamol tablets from his own bag. He so wanted her to start improving, but if anything, she seemed worse. He tried not to let his anxiety show.

"We have to give the antibiotics time to work; I am sure it won't be long before you begin to feel better. Morphine for pain and paracetamol to reduce the fever," he explained.

Annabel smiled but she was past caring and just held his hand as if afraid he might leave her.

"It's OK, better soon," he whispered.

Gradually she closed her eyes and fell asleep. He sat beside her until Mr Jasseri looked in to ask after the patient and to call him to supper. Rick was grateful for the whisky, but impatient to get back to Annabel.

That night Annabel's temperature rose higher than ever and paracetamol hardly touched it. The morphine made her drowsy and eventually she fell into a fitful sleep; she cried out and Rick got up and held her in his arms while he bathed her with tepid water all through the terrible, long night. In the morning, he was alarmed to see that she looked worse. Moreover, she was now delirious and the rash was more pronounced. He pulled on some clothes and went back to the main room where Mr J was having breakfast. In his anxious state, he forgot any preliminaries and sounded almost rude:

"We must get the doctor to come and see Annabel again. She seems worse to me. Perhaps the antibiotics aren't working."

His host agreed and Rick drove to fetch the physician. He put his foot down, shooting through the red lights. Traffic signals were a novelty to the drivers of Khorramabad; they pressed ahead regardless so Rick's

Road trip Isfahan 1969

driving did not attract attention. The doctor dropped everything to attend Annabel.

"She must not be moved," he declared, looking professionally concerned. "Typhoid often runs this course, but when the fever breaks she will quickly mend; she is young and fit, thank goodness."

More drugs were prescribed; Rick was not sure but it seemed likely that erythromycin was added and more morphine. He went off to get them, while Mr Jasseri's wife sat with her. Poor Annabel, she took the pills as soon as he got back without complaining and went to sleep. When she woke, her temperature was down but she was too ill to get into the shower.

"I feel so disgusting, please help me wash."

He picked her up and carried her into the shower, it was shocking how much weight she had lost in such a short time. She had never been heavy but now she felt as light as a kitten. Gently pulling her nightie over her head, he could not help noticing how prominent her ribs had become. He turned on the shower and stepped in holding her in his arms, tepid water poured over them both. Once she was dry, he fetched a clean nightie and dressed her.

"There we go Sugar! You'll soon be on the mend now."

Mr Jasseri took lunch at home. Today it was a huge feast of lamb and rice, followed by pears and melons. Rick had no appetite and wanted to get back to Annabel, but felt it would be rude to hurry away from the table.

The fever came back in the night but it wasn't as high and she did not become delirious again. Rick sat up with her holding her hand and making up stories:

Road trip Isfahan 1969

"We will drive away into the sunset and visit the exquisite mosques of Isfahan, we will drink only Canada Dry and eat only halva. And have long lie-ins in the morning, Sugar."

"Just thinking about it makes me feel exhausted. Can't we just stay here in bed for ever, Sugar?"

"We can't both be Sugar!"

"Well stop calling me Sugar then. It makes you sound like my Dad."

"I can tell you're on the mend."

She dosed off and he went back to his mattress in the corner.

Each day she was slightly stronger and able to eat a little more; she still had night sweats and a fever but they were gradually subsiding. It took another week before the doctor was convinced that Annabel was fit enough to go back to Baba Jan.

-§-

Everybody was pleased to see Annabel when the Land Rover arrived at camp. Sam hugged her.

"Please don't ever let anyone at home know how ill I have been, Rick."

"I won't. But you were so brave, I really admire your strength."

"And he was my guardian angel; weren't you, Sugar?"

"What's this Sugar business?" asked Sam.

"Oh nothing," replied Rick. "I was so worried when she was ill that I said some silly things. I'm sorry that I'm such a lousy nurse, Annabel."

Road trip Isfahan 1969

"He was hopeless, Sam. He put my nightie on back to front!"

"You let him dress you? Wow, you must have been feeling poorly."

-§-

It was Charles and Sam's last night. They were going to fly home from Tehran. This time the party was a more subdued affair and Annabel did not yet have the stamina to stay up late. However, the other two did seem to be getting on very well, Rick noticed. He and Annabel slipped away to their separate beds, hers in the house, his on the roof.

The next morning, they went up onto the tepi to say goodbye to the Prof and her team. The workmen were joking and singing. Their jokes consisted of counting to ten in English.

Bessart would shout: "one."

Rahaem would shout: "two."

Gomorrad would shout: "three."

When at last they got to ten, they burst out laughing.

They were saying their farewells when Rick noticed a procession moving slowly from the black tents towards the stream below the village. They appeared to be carrying a long bundle. It was the body of an old man; he was being carried down to the stream to be washed. Behind the men carrying the corpse walked his family and the rest of the village. The women were wailing and men were playing on pipes and drums. After a brief washing ritual, the deceased was wrapped in a white sheet and carried to the graveyard outside the village. He

Road trip Isfahan 1969

was laid to rest in a deep grave with stones on top of him. There were two large stones at either end of the mound of earth. The mourners daubed mud on their left sleeves and walked round and round the grave while the women went on wailing to the accompaniment of pipe and drum. Rick watched fascinated and oblivious to what was going on behind him.

"See you soon in Oxford," Annabel was saying to Charles who kissed her. That brought Rick back to earth. He was intensely annoyed. Sam distracted him by taking his head in her hands and kissing him on the lips.

"Good bye, old friend," she whispered, there were tears in her eyes.

"Safe journey," he replied, not trusting himself to say more.

-§-

Annabel and Rick did not talk much until they got to Khorramabad, he was lost in thought; he wished Charles had not kissed her like that. It implied that they were far more intimate than he realised. He felt uncomfortable, but they were going to be alone until they got back to Oxford. He could forget about Charles for the time being. Annabel was staring out of the window.

"What are you thinking about?"

"I'm thinking it's a long way home."

He laughed.

In Khorramabad, they stopped to buy the usual bread, eggs, fruit and vegetables and went to the Post Office so that Rick could mail the letters and cards he had written while Sam and the others were working on

Road trip Isfahan 1969

the tepi. At the bank, they changed Annabel's last few dollars, then they were on their way along a dirt track – the road to Isfahan.

Chapter Twelve
Baba Jan to Isfahan

They stopped late in the afternoon at a chai house. A truck that had been following them stopped too. The driver came over, sat down and ordered tea. At first they were wary, but he seemed friendly and spoke very good English. It turned out that he was an Armenian merchant on his way to Tehran.

"It is the custom in my country that travellers are always welcome," he told them in stilted English.

"Where are you coming from?" asked Annabel.

"Bandar Lengeh, it is a port on the Persian Gulf."

The driver explained he was taking his goods to market in the capital. The conversation dragged on, until the merchant announced that he had a long way to go. Rick tried to pay but the merchant insisted.

They turned off the main road and stopped under some trees by a stream. It was late and Annabel did not feel up to cooking, so they sat in the back of the Land Rover and ate cheese, tomatoes and apples.

Rick peeled the apple so that the skin came off in one long piece, and threw it over his shoulder. They turned and looked.

"That's an A alright," he said.

"If it is an A for Annabel then it's only a small a," she replied.

"You're only a small person."

"I'm average, actually."

"Believe me Annabel, there is nothing the least bit average about you."

Road trip Isfahan 1969

He leaned forwards as if he was going to kiss her. But she leant back:

"Aren't you going to put the tent up?"

"Can't you sleep in the front? I'll curl up here in the back."

"That's not very romantic!"

Rick agreed with her, but he did not imagine a night spent in the tent on camp-beds would be very romantic either. A plan was taking shape that he was sure Annabel would find romantic.

They woke before sunrise and fortified with coffee, set off for Isfahan. The mosques were visible in the distance across the dusty plain, silhouetted against the rising sun. Just as they approached the town, the muezzins climbed the minarets and started calling the faithful to prayer.

Prof. Goodchild had given them the address of her friend Henry, a school teacher and amateur archaeologist. She had written to warn him of the arrival of two students. He had agreed to put them up for a few days. They followed Prof's map and found the house in a residential part on the outskirts of town. He was out but his house keeper was expecting them and showed them into the main courtyard. Four separate bungalows surrounded the space just as at Mr Jasseri's house. One was for the women and another for the servants and the kitchen. Annabel was shown to a small room in the women's quarters and Rick was given a bed in the main bungalow.

They set off for the Friday Mosque which is the oldest, dating back to the 11th century. By now they knew the routine and were both suitably dressed. They

Road trip Isfahan 1969

removed their shoes and Annabel covered her head. The decorative tiles were stunning in detail and colour: intricate red and gold patterns. The cloisters around the mosque were cool and quiet. The central courtyard with its marble pool reflected the beauty of the building.

"This is so much more graceful and elegant than any of the mosques we have seen so far," whispered Rick.

"Yes, just amazing," said Annabel. "You don't have to whisper."

He put his arm around her waist and she didn't try to escape, but leant against his shoulder and looked up at tiled dome, sharply outlined against the deep blue sky.

They spent the rest of the day exploring the covered market. Rolls of the brightly coloured cloth were stacked up in front of a shop. In the back, the tailors and seamstresses were working away. A man came forward.

"Can I help you? Perhaps you would like me to make you a dress?"

Annabel smiled and shook her head, but Rick asked the man how long it would take.

"If I measure your wife now, she will have her dress by tomorrow evening."

"Really? How much will it cost?"

Annabel was talking to Rick and ignoring the salesman, but he butted in:

"Oh madam, for you it will only be a few rials and for a lady of such beauty, I myself will be willing to work all night."

"Go on Annabel, let him measure you up."

"But Rick, are you sure we can afford it?"

"Yes, and I'll have some trousers made. I can't go on wearing Sam's cast off jeans!"

Road trip Isfahan 1969

The deal was agreed and Annabel and Rick were measured up for their new clothes. They left the shop with much bowing, scraping and salaaming and continued to explore. Rick bought some alabaster beads from a stall and they peered into a workshop where children were making Persian carpets. Their tiny fingers flew over the loom, tying knot after knot with woollen and silk threads of different colours. There was an old man overseeing the work.

When they got back to Henry's house, he was waiting for them with tumblers of whisky.

"Supper will be ready in an hour. In the meantime, tell me about your adventures."

Annabel immediately told him about having a dress made. She was anxious that they were paying too much. When she mentioned the price, Henry laughed.

"That's a bargain. I know the shop. He is as honest as any tailor around here and you did well to find him. The dress will be lovely and I look forward to seeing you in it."

His bushy eyebrows shot up and he smiled.

"By the way, I have asked Tehrané to put you in the women's quarters. I wasn't sure if you two were an item?"

"Yes we are," said Rick.

"No we're not," said Annabel.

Henry looked from one to the other and burst out laughing. Annabel turned red and Rick did not know where to look.

"Well, if you go wandering about in the night no one will be shocked or surprised. But for the moment we will leave the arrangements as they are, shall we?"

Road trip Isfahan 1969

"Yes," said Rick.

"If Rick goes sneaking about in the night I will kill him, and any other intruders I come across. I always sleep with a dagger under my pillow!"

The bushy eyebrows shot up again and Henry laughed out loud. After a moment, all three regained their composure; it was time for supper: the usual mound of rice and chicken served on a huge round silver platter.

"Good night, you two! I am looking forward to showing you the sights tomorrow. You're a laugh a minute. I wonder what you will come up with next!"

Annabel disappeared off to the women's quarters and Rick went to his room feeling stupid. Annabel was right when she denied they were lovers, but that made him even more determined to win her over. On reflection, he decided against trying to find his way to the women's quarters in the dark.

They stayed with Henry for two days, exploring the mosques and the markets. The Imam Mosque was even more beautiful than the Friday Mosque, tiles even richer in colour: blue and gold, but the most extraordinary of all was the Shiek Lotfollah Mosque: the impressive tiled dome was decorated in blue and green and of course, gold. The tiles depicted flowers and birds. Henry was an amazing fund of knowledge about ancient Persia, and told them of caves on the Caspian Sea that they should visit.

Henry had to go back to work next day, so Annabel and Rick, now familiar with the layout of the streets went back to the tailor and she tried on the dress. It fitted perfectly; she looked stunning. A twirl made the dress float up, showing her knees.

Road trip Isfahan 1969

"How do I look?"

"OK."

Annabel's face fell and Rick thought she was going to cry. Oblivious to the seamstresses and others in the shop he stepped forward and took her in his arms.

"You look stunning and I want you.... you can't imagine how much."

He planted a clumsy kiss on her nose and then another on her mouth.

She wrapped her arms so tightly around his neck that he couldn't breathe and then kissed him back.

"You are such a bastard!"

The people in the shop burst into applause.

They wandered away from the shop, swinging their parcels. Turning into a wide street they found themselves in front of a modern looking hotel that obviously catered for tourists. On the spur of the moment they went in.

"What are we doing here?"

"Just wait Annabel, I have a surprise for you."

He went up to the desk and booked a room for the night.

"Will you be dining here, Sir?"

In his excitement Rick hadn't thought about dinner, he nodded and grinned.

They went back to Henry's and as soon as he came home told him they were leaving for Tehran right away. He did seem rather surprised. Annabel gave him a bunch of dates and a card.

"Thank you so much for looking after us," she said and standing on tiptoe kissed him.

They drove the Land Rover round to the hotel and a bell boy took Annabel's suitcase and Rick's rucksack up

Road trip Isfahan 1969

to their room. The first thing they noticed was the bed; it was an enormous four-poster surrounded by net curtains.

"I didn't know there were mosquitoes here," said Rick.

"There aren't, those are not mosquito nets, there're drapes. Very tasteful!"

"Oh, silly me." Rick was feeling nervous.

It seemed strange to be sitting in the dining room, in their new clothes, eating a three-course meal, but it was a change from ratatouille, and at least there were no sheep's eyeballs, as Rick pointed out, he went on:

"You're so pretty in your new dress: it suits you!"

"Rick! I am amazed you even noticed. What's got into you?"

"Don't tease, you know how much I …. um…. er ….admire you."

"No, you never said. How was I to know?"

Rick decided attack was the best form of defence:

"What are you wearing under your dress?"

"Wouldn't you like to know!"

"Well, I'm imagining French knickers."

"And?"

"No bra, you never wear a bra."

"And you know I haven't any French knickers."

"I'll buy you some when we get to Paris."

"And until then I'll be knicker-less?"

He started to giggle and she joined in.

Fortified by wine, coffee and a strange liqueur, they went back to the hall. The lift seemed to take a long time to come. Suddenly Annabel picked up her skirts and made a dash for the stairs.

"Race you!" she called.

Road trip Isfahan 1969

They arrived in the room panting and laughing. He threw her on the bed and started to undo the buttons on the back of her dress.

"Stop, stop. You'll ruin my new frock."

She knelt on the bed and he stood behind her. She lifted her arms and he pulled it over her head. She was completely naked.

"Annabel! What happened to your underwear?"

He was stunned by how beautiful she looked in the evening light slanting through the window. She turned slowly round and helped him undress, but still held him at arm's length.

"Now say it."

"Say what?"

He was in a hurry and didn't catch her meaning.

"Say how much you admire me."

The penny dropped at last.

"I love you Annabel. I have loved you from the moment we met!"

"You lying toad. But I do believe you love me now."

She put her arms around his neck and pulled him to her.

They fell onto the bed; she lay completely motionless while he caressed her. Then in characteristic Annabel fashion, quick as a flash, with no warning, like a tiger going for its prey, she rolled him over and jumped on top.

-§-

They lay wrapped in each other's arms.

Road trip Isfahan 1969

"I was worried I wouldn't be any good," she whispered.

"But you were….um…. amazing," Rick struggled to find the right word.

"Yes, just absolutely amazing."

He kissed her.

She smiled up at him, her large blue eyes gazing into his:

"You're just rubbish, though; I did all the work!"

She shut her eyes and began to shake with silent laughter.

He knew she was teasing and rolled on top of her.

"Practice can only make perfect, Annabel!"

-§-

In the morning Rick went to pay the bill at the desk. Just as they were leaving who should walk in but Henry.

"Fancy seeing you two here!"

He did not seem that surprised. Rick and Annabel stood side by side holding hands and feeling rather like two naughty sixth formers.

"I knew you were lovers as soon as I saw you, but I didn't want to presume or offend. I do hope you will come back to Isfahan soon."

Rick shook his hand and Annabel kissed him and they followed the bell boy out to the Land Rover.

That night when they pulled off the road Annabel did the cooking: fried eggs and tomatoes. Rick put up the tent and arranged the camp-beds side by side. At last they were alone with no one to bother them and the luxury of endless conversation without interruption. He

Road trip Isfahan 1969

wanted to help Annabel undress again, but she shooed him out of the tent and only called to him when she was safely in bed. He slipped into his sleeping bag, then leaning over unzipped hers and was just admiring her knees when the camp-bed capsized and he fell onto the ground sheet. She looked down on him smiling. She was wearing her usual T-shirt, but now she peeled it off and pitched forwards on top of him.

"Oh, Annabel!"

-§-

They tried to go to sleep on one camp-bed but that proved impossible; it was easier to sleep on the ground on a pile of blankets, with one sleeping bag under them and one over them.

"Penny for your thoughts?"

"I was wondering, Annabel…. Er….I hope…. I mean I hope you don't get pregnant."

"I hope YOU don't get me pregnant, it's not just up to me you know."

"Yes, but are you safe? I mean, you are on the pill aren't you?"

"No, I'm not. You're my first boyfriend. And I was not planning on anything like this happening. I was relying on you to know what to do."

"I do love you so much Annabel; I don't want anything to go wrong."

"Well at the moment I'm safe, I think. I've only just finished my period, so your timing was quite good, or lucky. But you must take precautions, lover."

Road trip Isfahan 1969

"Rhythm method? I don't think that's very reliable, do you?"

"Well we will just have to hope it works, won't we?"

"No, no. I'll sort something out when we get to Tehran, I'm just as worried as you are. But there wasn't anywhere to get anything in Khorramabad. And anyway I wasn't sure you would want to be my girlfriend! Not even when I was booking the hotel."

Road trip Isfahan 1969

Chapter Thirteen
Tehran to the Caspian Sea

They arrived in Tehran in the middle of rush hour. It was like driving in London or any modern capital city; the pace was hectic and it was hard to find anyone who could tell them how to get to the British Institute. But when at last they arrived, it was a haven of peace and quiet. David S was very kind and offered them tea (Earl Grey). They asked him about the excavations at Babol Sar. He knew all about the caves and gave them very useful directions. The main thing was that letters had arrived for them both. Annabel's were full of good wishes from her mother and the rest of the family with heart-felt advice:

"Stay safe and be careful, darling."

Rather more to the point, Rick's letter contained a £10 note.

"Ha ha," said Rick "this should just about get us home?"

Annabel looked doubtful:

"Now I know it is so easy, I will send a begging letter to my mum. I don't think £10 will even pay for enough petrol to get us home, will it?"

"There are still some travellers' cheques left, so we'll be OK."

"We should not have been so extravagant in Isfahan."

He put his arms around her and squeezing her tight, kissed her on the mouth.

Road trip Isfahan 1969

"I do so love you," he said and added. "I am going to get a haircut; will you wait here, in the canteen?"

Annabel looked puzzled but when he explained to her that women would not be welcome in a Persian barber's shop, she let him go.

The owner of the place finished cutting Rick's hair and shaving off his stubble, as if he were a cowboy just ridden into town, and then, as Rick paid up, he asked, like barbers do all over the world: "Anything for the week end, sir?"

There were rows and rows of Durex on a low shelf discretely placed behind the counter. Rick leaned over to scrutinise what was on offer but he was not at all sure which ones to choose, so he went for the cherry flavoured and the tickler.

"How many packets, Sir?"

Rick held up both hands with fingers spread. The man smiled and handed them over.

"Plenty jigajig! You very lucky man."

"Allah be praised," replied Rick and nearly ran out of the shop.

-§-

The road climbed steeply into the mountains. Ahead were snow-covered peaks. A landslide blocked the road and traffic took to a bumpy improvised detour. The truck drivers were complete maniacs, and overtook at every opportunity, round bends and even into the mouths of tunnels. Annabel remained surprisingly calm. Rick could not look at her, it was all he could do to keep them from

Road trip Isfahan 1969

being pushed off the road and down the mountainside. Then they were over the watershed.

"Wow," said Annabel

The Elburz Mountains facing the Caspian Sea were emerald green, with tall trees that looked like oaks and green grass that they had not seen since leaving Yugoslavia. It was an astonishing change from the dusty arid brown of the country on the landward side of the mountains.

It was dark by the time they arrived at Babol Sar, weaving through cyclists, pedestrians and horses which emerged out of the gloom with alarming lack of respect for traffic.

They set up camp on the beach and immediately went for a swim in the dark, stark naked.

"Don't go too far out, Annabel."

"I won't abandon you, lover."

She came towards him as graceful as a dolphin and just as playful. They hugged in the shallows. It was so lovely and cool after a sweltering day on the road.

"We've swum in the rivers of the Dordogne, the Aegean, the Black Sea, the rivers of Iran and now the Caspian Sea."

Annabel hung around his neck and kissed him: "Paddled in your case," she corrected him.

It was a happy moment. They went back to the tent and dried off, changed their clothes and settled down to Minestrone soup and melon. As Annabel was getting ready for bed she asked Rick:

"What does PP stand for?"

"Er…what did you say?"

Road trip Isfahan 1969

Rick had to think fast. She repeated the question, and he swallowed hard.

"Sam told me your nick name was PP."

"That Sam, she never could keep a secret," Rick mumbled.

"But why is it a secret and what does it stand for?"

"OK I'll tell you. But first promise that there will never ever be any secrets between us."

"Go on," Annabel urged.

"Promise."

"OK I promise."

"Well it stands for Priapic Prince; there I've told now." Rick felt embarrassed, but much worse was to come.

"Wait a minute! What were you two doing? I mean were you kissing her? Did she have her hand in your pants?"

"Why did she tell you her nickname for me?" Rick asked.

"Forget that. You have been having sex with her, haven't you?"

"NO, I promise you: we did not have sex."

"Well what did you do with her?"

"Please Annabel, believe me, there never was anything like that between us."

"There must have been. Was it the night of the party?"

"Ok I'll tell you what happened when I saw you kissing Charles."

"I never kissed Charles."

"No lies, no secrets remember. I saw you on the roof."

Road trip Isfahan 1969

"OK I kissed him once, but what were you up to with Sam?"

"We kissed; I wanted you, but you were kissing Charles. I knew you'd met in Oxford, and I thought you were lovers."

It all came out in a rush, all the awful jealous thoughts he had had that night which he thought justified his behaviour with Sam.

But Annabel hadn't finished: "You're a liar! I'm sure your hands were all over her and I bet she was busy undressing you, you bastard!"

She was shouting now; Rick cowered away as she came at him with, claws and teeth. He held her wrists.

"And I bet Charles was more than just kissing you."

Bad move, Rick, he heard Sam's voice telling him. Annabel let out a scream that echoed into the night and broke free from him.

"How dare you!"

She grabbed her things and ran over to the Land Rover and locked herself in. Rick was appalled. Panic stopped him thinking clearly; he could hardly breathe. What a fool, he should have said something different, anything, but what? Rick spent the night wondered how he was going to redeem himself. He slept badly.

-§-

Next morning Annabel seemed to have calmed down. She let him pass her a cup of tea through the window. In total silence, they drove towards Behshahr and the caves. The atmosphere was heavy and humid; it felt like rain. The coastal strip was very flat, a flood plain with great

Road trip Isfahan 1969

clumps of bamboo and other water loving plants. At last they found the cave.

"This must be the one David called Con's Cave," said Rick.

Annabel got down on her knees and picked up a few fragments of pottery.

"These cave dwellers had great views over the lagoon to the sea," Rick noted, trying to sound casual, but inside he was hurt and frustrated. He felt Annabel had cut herself off from him.

Annabel looked over her shoulder out to the Caspian but still said nothing. Not speaking they drove back to Behshahr, and bought the usual supplies. David S had told them about another place, called MacBurney's cave. They asked for directions and the shop keeper detailed two boys to accompany them. At the end of a narrow farm track, they came at last to the cave. It had been meticulously excavated in layers.

"You can see the hearth where the Bronze Age people cooked, at least 4000 years ago," said Rick.

The boys offered them some wild figs and blackberries. Annabel smiled and thanked them in Farsi. They left and she handed some to Rick; sitting overlooking the sea they ate the fruit. Rick wanted to say something but the words would not come. He wanted to be friends again, he had no hope that they would ever be lovers.

Heading west through Sari back towards Babol Sar, they passed houses that were thatched with reeds and built on stilts to keep them above the flood water. The rain came pouring down.

"Where to next?" asked Rick.

Road trip Isfahan 1969

Annabel unfolded the map. "After Babol Sar we take the road to Chalus. Looks like a good camping spot up ahead."

As they parked up, some Persian students shot past in their camper van and stuck fast in the mud. Rick went over to see if he could help but despite revving the engine and spinning the wheels the van did not move. He went back to the Land Rover where the resourceful Annabel had already arranged the back so that she could cook the evening meal of fried eggs and tomatoes. Rick watched her and sadly thought that ratatouille seemed to be something from the distant past, in the days when they were at least friends.

Annabel slept on the front seat and Rick crept into the back. The rain continued to drench everything.

Rick was up at first light, and went for a swim in the sea, then made coffee and handed it in through the window to Annabel; she smiled at him and opened her mouth to say something just as the Persian students came running over. They explained that a man with a tractor was coming to tow them back onto the road.

It started to rain again as they passed Chalus and climbed up through the mountains towards Tehran. The lush vegetation was still something of a novelty, but as soon as they were over the pass the climate changed back to arid desert. They left the snow-capped mountains behind and descended to the plain. Suddenly Annabel spoke:

"He did touch me. I was just too embarrassed to tell you. I'm sorry Rick. But you weren't my boyfriend then and I didn't feel I was being disloyal. It wasn't anything serious and all the time I wanted to be with you."

Road trip Isfahan 1969

Rick closed his eyes and the Land Rover nearly left the road. He felt so grateful for this confession that concentration was for a moment impossible. He turned onto a dirt track and stopped.

"Oh Annabel, you were just as muddled as I was!"

He started kissing her all over her face and neck. She laughed, pulled up her T-shirt and let him kiss her breasts. They bundled out onto the ground and he began to undress.

"Not so fast. We can't make love here and now, not even this month."

"Yes we can; I've got some things."

But he could not remember where the "things" were. Annabel came up with a solution, and they could get underway again.

"Goodness me Annabel, you are full of surprises. Where did you learn tricks like that?"

"Well you said no secrets, so I'll tell you, but you must promise not to be shocked: Sam told me what to do......Why have you gone bright red?"

"Well no secrets and please don't hit me. It was like with you and Charles, I did not want Sam to be offended so well...."

"She did it to you?"

Annabel looked surprised, but this time not angry. She started to laugh. "We wanted each other but Sam and Charles cruelly took advantage of our kind natures," she said.

"You certainly have a way with words Annabel; I really love you. I'll never be unfaithful."

Road trip Isfahan 1969

"But you're a man, aren't you? So, at the first opportunity you will be off with any tart that takes your fancy."

"Don't tease, you're not a tart, you are my first girlfriend, and I promise not to let you go. You wouldn't dump me for a gorilla, would you?"

"Are you saying Charles is a gorilla?"

"Yes, and you are much too good for him, he's a self-centred bastard."

"I love you Rick and I trust you, but you are so naive."

"And you're not?"

"No."

Annabel smiled and left Rick wondering what on earth she could be thinking. They drove on in silence but now the sun was out and she was stroking his thigh.

-§-

Approaching Tehran they passed an emerald green reservoir where people were water skiing.

"Wow, I never expected to see that in Persia," said Rick.

"Clearly there are parts of Persia that are extremely wealthy," Annabel replied.

They stopped for a lunch of bread and cheese in a chai house. The owner directed them to a campsite outside Tehran. It was luxurious, with its own swimming pool and restaurant. There was even a laundry. They gave their dirty washing to the attendant and went for a swim. The other campers were all Persian but dressed in European style.

Road trip Isfahan 1969

"Clearly this is where Tehran's jet set come to play. Do you think we are smart enough?" asked Annabel.

"I'm not sure, it is all so different from Khorramabad," answered Rick.

They lay on sun-loungers by the pool and snoozed away the afternoon. Rick roused himself and went to get their clothes from the washerwoman.

"It cost 80 rials," he told Annabel.

"You're frittering our money away, Rick."

"But it's worth it to have clean clothes to put on for a change."

Swimming in the moonlight made the perfect end to a day that had started badly and finished full of promise. Rick made the tent look as inviting as he could by arranging rugs and cushions like something from the Arabian Nights. He lit a joss stick.

"Looks and smells like a tart's boudoir," said Annabel.

"Are you complaining?"

Rick got out his purchases from the barber.

"What's that?" Annabel asked.

She took the cherry flavoured one and blew it up; it slipped out of her fingers and shot out of the tent. She laughed so much that Rick gave up and they fell asleep in each other's arms as innocent as the day they were born.

Road trip Isfahan 1969

Chapter Fourteen
Tehran to Istanbul

The wind was making the tent flap like a bird about to take off. Rick left Annabel in her sleeping bag and went off to the showers. When he returned with coffee she was not grateful.

"What time do you call this? I want my lie-in."

She snuggled down, and pulled Rick on top of her. She whispered in his ear.

"Balloons?" he asked her.

"Yes, and this time I won't laugh."

-§-

In Tehran, they caught up with David S to tell him about their trip. There was a letter for Annabel from her mother. Inside were two £10 notes.

"Wow, that is generous."

"You can thank my mum in person when we get home."

"What will she say when she finds out her daughter has a boyfriend?"

"Oh, she will probably kill you, if my brother doesn't."

"No need to worry then. What if I said I wanted to marry you?"

"She would just kick you in the balls, for being so stupid."

"Would your mother do a thing like that? Even if I told her that I would soon be rich and famous?"

Road trip Isfahan 1969

"A. You do not know the women in my family. B. You would be lying."

"Well, you may be right there Annabel."

"Boring, boring!" she said.

Rick felt confused, was she mocking him?

"Stop it, Annabel."

He stood in front of her, put both hands on her shoulders, and held her gaze; she relaxed into his arms and let him kiss her.

They headed out of Tehran on the road to Tabriz. A cold north wind was blowing from the snow-capped mountains over the flat plane that lay ahead. The gale quickly turned into a dust storm.

"Can you see anything at all, Rick?"

"Enough, we've got to keep going."

"Stop at the next village, I need a drink and I don't want to squat behind a bush in these conditions."

Any hope of pitching the tent had to be abandoned and they cooked and slept in the Land Rover. It was hopeless trying to share the back so Annabel slept on the front seat.

"No romance for you tonight, Rick!"

"This is no honeymoon, is it? Never mind, Annabel, when we get to Istanbul we will give ourselves a treat."

"Can't wait!"

They were getting into more mountainous country, with fields that were being ploughed by oxen with wooden ploughs that had not changed in thousands of years. There were flocks of sheep and goats and a lonely camel, saddled up, waiting for his master to return. The wind had died down, but it was still cold as they made their way to Tabriz, the last town before the frontier.

Road trip Isfahan 1969

-§-

On the Persian side of the boarder formalities were quickly completed, but on the Turkish side there seemed to be a riot going on. Customs officers and soldiers were battling a hoard of hippies who seemed to have gone mad and were lashing out indiscriminately. One picked up a stone and threw it at the Land Rover.

"Rick!" screamed Annabel. "Get us out of here."

He reversed and they left in a cloud of dust, stopping at the first chai house to wait for things to calm down.

"Blimey that was nasty. I wonder what's making the hippies so angry," he said.

"They're probably loaded with opium and hash from India and Afghanistan and the custom officers are trying to confiscate it," Annabel replied.

"Looks to me like they are out of their minds on the stuff." said Rick.

"You were so cool back there," she said. "You didn't even blink when I screamed."

Once the hippies had moved on, or been imprisoned, they returned to the Customs House and helped a soldier to put their names into a huge ledger. He seemed very merry and laughed a lot. But the mood changed when he took Annabel into another room and told Rick to stay in the Land Rover. It was not clear what was going on, there was at least a possibility that something unpleasant was about to happen. Rick got out of the Land Rover and moved towards the entrance, but was barred by another soldier, who gestured to him to wait. The soldier cradled his rifle and watched him with a completely impassive

Road trip Isfahan 1969

face, clearly he was not impressed with the English and it would not take much to get them both locked up. When Annabel re-appeared, she looked upset.

"What went on in there?"

"I thought I was going to be strip searched, but I did my best to stay calm. They asked me if we had any contraband and then one of the soldiers patted me all over. I was scared, Rick."

"What happened next?'

"A man who looked like an officer appeared and they let me go. They did look a bit sheepish."

"Goodness Annabel, that was a narrow escape. I was imagining all sorts of things but did not know what to do. What could we do against soldiers with guns?"

"You could have strangled them with your bare hands, or don't you love me that much?"

"No, probably not. But if you died I would die too, just to be with you."

"What a liar, you are! I knew I could never rely on you to protect me."

They were driving down a dusty road towards Agri, so he couldn't take her in his arms at that moment and kiss her to tell her how worried he had been and how much he loved her. The sun was setting; they pulled off the road and drove up a track to a place screened by a wood. He wrapped himself around her skinny body and they made love in the back of the Land Rover.

"Awe Rick, you should have bought a long wheel base jobby. This is too cramped."

"Right Annabel, but how was I to know you would be so hot, and the nights would be so cold up here in the mountains?"

Road trip Isfahan 1969

They tried to make up a bed for two but it was just impossible and it was freezing so there was no way they could sleep in the tent; Rick moved to the front seat. They knelt and kissed over the backrest like frustrated lovers in a Shakespearian play.

-§-

The dawn woke them early and since Annabel was in the back it was her turn to make the coffee. In Erzurum, they went to change money in one of the main banks. Unfortunately, when it came to changing Persian rials into Turkish lira they got about two thirds of what they expected. Annabel handed over two thousand rials and got back 200 lira. They knew that in Iran £10 was worth two thousand rials, but the bank would only give the equivalent of £5. Arguing with the cashier was hopeless, not least because of the language barrier.

"We should have taken into account that changing American dollars or pounds sterling for local currency gives a vastly better exchange rate than changing one local currency for another," said Annabel.

Rick just shook his head:

"Whatever we do we seem to get robbed. We needed to change the £10 pound note into rials; they wouldn't change any less. It's not your fault."

"I know that! But we have still lost at least £5, when we need to be careful of every penny."

They left Erzurum feeling fed up and depressed. The sun was going down behind the trees in a deep valley; they turned off the road up a cart track and bumped across some scrubby grass to camp by a river. It was too

Road trip Isfahan 1969

cold to swim but they walked along by the water, each lost in thought. It seemed an awfully long way home. After another uncomfortable night in the Land Rover, they woke to the squeaking of wheels of a bullock cart as it went creaking on its way up the track into the hills. The owner was walking beside the animals. It was a peaceful and timeless scene, soothing and somehow reassuring after the recent setbacks.

-§-

After that sunrise followed sunset in a steady routine until at last they left the mountains and camped by the seashore outside Izmit.

"Here we are back where we camped on our first night in Turkey. I'll pitch the tent and we'll have a proper camp and a good night's sleep," said Rick, spreading cushions about so that the tent looked like a Seraglio.

Annabel however had other ideas; she whispered her thoughts in Rick's ear. He looked intrigued.

"I love your dirty mind; I love everything about you."

What had he done to deserve Annabel, and what in him had turned a rather standoffish blue-stocking into such a wild lover?

-§-

They were at the port by 10.00am and had breakfast sitting in the Land Rover. The trip across the Bosphorus was quick, the ferries frequent and efficient. They drove

Road trip Isfahan 1969

through Istanbul taking the route that ran along beside the sea.

"We're back in Europe, Rick."

"So we are Annabel!"

"Let's find that campsite."

While Annabel was in the showers, Rick went off to the café/shop and bumped into a friend from school. Josh did look different: the last time Rick had seen him he was a school boy in uniform with the regulation haircut. Now his greasy hair hung to his shoulders, his beard was long and unkempt. The sun had burnt his face to a dark brown and he was wearing a white embroidered shirt that hung to his knees. There were blue beads hanging around his neck.

The shop had a veranda with tables and chairs. They sat down with a bottle of wine and a bag of pistachio nuts. There was so much to say, so much to catch up. They swapped lies about their travels. Josh was on his way back to Cambridge where he was in his last year reading English. But he was not going to stay in England, having spent the summer in India he planned to return to immerse himself in the mystic secrets of yoga. Rick felt very boring and conservative; all he could offer in return was tales from medical school. He felt dull and pedestrian.

Back at the tent Annabel had done the washing and hung it out to dry.

"I am starving," she announced.

Josh invited himself to the gigantic fry-up, and contributed a bottle of retsina. He completely dominated the conversation with egocentric stories before wandering off. Annabel watched him go:

Road trip Isfahan 1969

"A pseudo-intellectual of the first water, boasting about his plans to study yoga and write novels and all the usual stuff. I am so unimpressed."

"You sound quite cross."

"There are just so many undergraduates like him hanging around every campus hoping to seduce women with their grand ideas, and trying at the same time to belittle their rivals. He has no idea how ridiculous he looks."

Rick moved towards her and started to say something but she stopped him.

"Why," she demanded, "were you apologising to a pseud like that?"

"I don't have your confidence, or your brains."

She snorted.

"I would love to be a writer and an actor; a star of stage and screen, rich and famous. If only I had his talent."

Annabel laughed out loud. "Don't be ridiculous."

"Well, what do you want to do after you have left Oxford?" Rick asked.

"Why do you think I'll ever leave Oxford?"

"Well, after you have got your degree, then."

"I'll probably get a research post in the department, and teach."

"Like your mum and dad, teach Classics for the rest of your life?"

Annabel was silent. Absentmindedly she looked around for the corkscrew and opened another bottle of wine, she splashed some into his glass but did not look up. She looked so serious that Rick began to think he had said something wrong. She lay back on the cushions and

Road trip Isfahan 1969

Rick settled down beside her. Still not looking at him she began to talk as if arguing with herself.

"I'm almost scared of going home now. Of course, I want to see my tutor and get back to my studies, but I feel I've changed; maybe I won't be able to relate to them like I did before, maybe it won't seem so interesting. You've altered the way I see things, at first I thought you were just a rather boring person with no more ambition than to follow in the footsteps of the rest of your family. But now I see you're different, and I admire you and I'm grateful that you're so practical and have managed to get us this far with no major disasters. Maybe there is more to life than researching and punting."

"Punting on the Cherwell? Supine I raised my knees on the floor of a narrow punt?"

Annabel pounced on him:

"You really are an unfeeling Philistine. And you've totally screwed up that quote from Eliot. It was not the Cherwell River; it was the Thames and it was a canoe not a punt. Just as I was pouring my heart out to you. You bastard."

Rick pinned her down and after a brief struggle she let him kiss her.

"Annabel I just love you so much and I want to say that I have changed too but I don't have the words to tell you…. Scrambled eggs for supper, just to make a change?"

"Blokes! Dogs have more feeling!"

-§-

Road trip Isfahan 1969

The next morning, they lay side by side in the tent reading and scratching their mosquito bites.

"We've got to get money from the British Consulate," said Rick. "If we don't get funds somehow we won't have enough money for petrol let alone food on the way home."

"I told you we should not be so extravagant, when we were in Isfahan.

"You didn't want to lose your virginity in the back of a Land Rover, did you?"

"I am ignoring that coarse remark. When we get married I will take charge of the finances, as well as our social life."

"Are we getting married? Oh, Annabel! But what about your mother kicking me in the balls. I want to avoid that if at all possible, and as for your brother well...."

"You're getting ahead of yourself; you're not rich and famous yet."

He pulled her down and kissed her.

"We'll get married anyway, whether I'm rich and famous or not....won't we?"

"How do I know?" Annabel looked sad.

"It's easy to get carried away when we're so far from home. I'm missing my own bed and my family, Rick. Take me back where I belong."

She rolled over, planted both elbows on his stomach and stared into his eyes.

-§-

Road trip Isfahan 1969

In the old part of Istanbul, they found the British Consulate and were directed to a queue of students wanting funds to get home. In front of them was a girl in flared jeans, an embroidered waistcoat and a straw hat; her dirty blonde hair hung down her back. There was an aroma of cannabis. When she got to the window behind which sat the official with the power to say yea or nay, she boldly announced that she needed funds to travel to Katmandu. A long discussion followed the gist of which was that funds were for repatriation not for going further afield. In the end, she gave up and it was Rick's turn. He explained that they did not have enough money for fuel to get home.

"No problem, Sir."

Rick wrote a cheque made out to CFFO for £45. The clerk gave them a chit to be changed at a bank.

"Give the chitty to me, lover."

"Here you are, but don't forget I am the one who wrote the cheque."

"And I'm the one in charge now," Annabel said.

"If I'd known I would have brought the Rolls, mi lady.

"Pink?"

"Of course Lady P."

"What does P stand for?"

"Panties."

Annabel swiped him round the head.

"I wish I had my riding whip now. You'd be begging me for mercy."

They went trucking down the street singing the song made popular by Aretha Franklin.

Road trip Isfahan 1969

By now it was midday and they stopped for baklava and yogurt; when the bank opened, they opted for US dollars. The chit was worth $100. Dollars would hold their value better than any other currency; and they did not want to repeat the experience they had when entering Turkey.

"Next stop - Topkapi Palace."

"Oh Rick I am so excited. To think you promised we'd see the Palace on the way back. Thank you, thank you."

She hung around his neck kissing him.

The walls were battered and broken but in 1453 they had allowed the Christians to defy Mehmed II for almost two months before the city was finally taken.

"Don't talk to me Rick. In fact, stay out of sight, I want to really take this all in."

He loitered behind her at a respectful distance.

First impressions were of vast courtyards containing fountains and trees; the guidebook told them that caravans would come into the palace and camp in these outer courtyards while the leader waited for an audience with the Sultan. As they went on, the courtyards became smaller and more intimate with steps leading up to wall-top walks with views over the city and across the Bosphorus to Asia. There was a small but beautifully decorated mosque reserved for the women. The scent of various flowering shrubs filled the air even at this late time of year. Ante-rooms and chambers led up to the throne room. The display cases contained enormous jewels and sumptuous robes as well as pottery and porcelain from around the world. There were displays of daggers and swords and other bizarre treasures such as

Road trip Isfahan 1969

parts of John the Baptist, including his skull, and the sword and cloak of Mohammed the Prophet.

"Can I speak now?" Rick asked.

"What do you want to say?"

"Wow!"

"Anything else?"

"Yes, let's stop for a cup of tea."

"And baklava?" she asked.

"Anything for you my sweet."

"Don't you my sweet me."

-§-

They left the coffee shop and crossed a courtyard. "Now for the harem," said Rick.

"I can't get my head around the idea that beautiful and intelligent women could have been locked up here until they died. It's really horrendous," said Annabel.

They moved through cool rooms with high ceilings wonderfully decorated with tiles. One could imagine the Sultan and his courtiers lounging on divans covered with richly embroidered cushions while the women and girls from the harem entertained them.

"It may not have been that bad, many moved on to become the wives of one of the many Pashas or provincial rulers. If one was extremely ambitious and luck was on your side you might become the mother of the next Sultan, the Valide Sultan, the second most powerful person in the Empire."

"How could you say that Rick! I'm disgusted that you could say such a thing. These women were treated

Road trip Isfahan 1969

like cattle, it was a degrading, humiliating existence; there is no possible justification."

Rick was taken aback, at school and in the history books and indeed in the guide book in his hand, the harem and the concubines who lived out their lives here, were just a fact of life. He was mortified by his own insensitivity.

"Never underestimate women, Rick, even in the most unpromising circumstances one or two have made it to the top: look at Eleanor of Aquitaine or Emma Hamilton or Marie Curie. You cannot excuse the barbarous practice of keeping women in a harem by claiming that one or two women overcame all the odds. What about all those who were sold on or discarded in other ways when they were no longer useful?"

Rick was silent. He looked at the ground.

"And look what the guide book says about the eunuchs who guarded the women!"

Annabel's eyes were out on storks and she was getting even more angry.

"Even though Islam forbids the castration of boys, that did not stop the servants of the Sultan buying them from the Coptic monks of Abyssinia. I've had enough Rick! I feel sick; come on let's go."

They walked fast, Annabel not looking where she was going, Rick anxiously steering her back towards the café they had visited with Sam. They sat side by side on a bench seat.

"A lot of water has flowed under the bridge since we were last here; I never thought then that we would become such good friends," said Rick.

Road trip Isfahan 1969

"I don't want to be friends. If you can't love me for ever, I'll kill you."

Rick reached out to tickle her, but she grabbed his hand and pressed it to her lips, and bit it.

"Ow, tiger."

She smiled like a cat and stretched out a paw to rake her claws through his stubbly beard. Not quite sure what to expect he grabbed her wrist, pulled her to him and kissed her. He went off to pay at the till, feeling like a millionaire.

They drove slowly along beside the sea until they got to the beach by the camp. Annabel swam out for what seemed like miles leaving Rick trailing in her wake. Then she duck-dived and swam underneath him, as he struggled back to the beach she did it again and again. Standing in the shallows Rick caught his breath:

"Annabel! You have no idea what the sight of you duck-diving does to me."

"Oh?"

She laughed.

Chapter Fifteen
Istanbul to Oxford

It was time to hurry home, to get back to university and re-join the real world. Rick checked over the Land Rover, and Annabel loaded the last of their stuff into the back. It took four hours to reach the border, over bumpy roads. The Turkish border guards not surprisingly took them for hippies and assumed that they had cannabis on board. They made them completely unload the Land Rover. Clothes, sleeping bags and cooking utensils were strewn all over the place. Then they started to search each of them individually. Annabel kept close to Rick.

"Don't let them separate us," she whispered.

He held her hand, feeling anxious and unsure what to do. It was only later he realised that sweat was running off the tips of his fingers.

However, the guards lost interest and indicated they could go. Wiping his hands on his shorts he climbed into the driver's seat and drove along to the Greek customs officer who dismissed them with a casual wave of a gloved hand. 30km further on in Alexandroupoli they stopped to buy eggs, bread and cheese, tomatoes, oil and wine.

"We need money for fuel, Annabel."

"I'll cash a $10 travellers' cheque, while you re-fuel."

They slept out under the stars that night, on their camp-beds, holding hands, gazing up at the heavens. It was one of those moments when souls melt into one another and become part of the universe.

Road trip Isfahan 1969

The next morning Rick was up first and made coffee.
"Come on sleepy head, time to rise and shine."

Annabel rubbed her eyes, reached for her glasses and focused on her lover.

"Ah there you are! You haven't gone without me."
"Never."

He took her glasses off her nose and kissed her, she pulled him down and rolled off the camp-bed, landing on top of him. Rick was lost in another world, overwhelmed by her passion.

"I'm too tired to drive now."

"Come on; a swim will revive you."

They passed through Komotini and in Xanthi took the mountain road out of the town, making a detour past Kavala. The olives were being harvested on hillside terraces.

"Always the scenic route, as Jon would say."

"You know I love the scenic route, Rick."

She stroked his thigh and leant against him. On the way to the border they stopped only once to fill up with petrol and were through customs and in Yugoslavia by 4pm. There were no dramas this time. At the top of a winding wooded valley, they found a flat place to camp on the banks of the river. Rick noted in his journal: "And so to bed. Last night to the sound of the Aegean, tonight to the sound of a river."

Yugoslavia did not seem so bleak on the way back. The road meandered through woods and mountains. After Skopje, the road became a major highway and they made very good time to Belgrade.

"We'll soon be home at this rate," Annabel smiled.

Road trip Isfahan 1969

"Not too soon I hope. I want to keep you all to myself."

Annabel pushed her hand under his shirt and tried to tickle him.

"Stop, stop! You'll have us in the ditch!"

"Spoil sport!"

-§-

They were sitting at a table on the pavement outside a rather grand café on the wide and fashionable boulevard in Belgrade, when acquaintances of Annabel's from Oxford turned up. Rick didn't know these guys but it seemed that Annabel had been at school with one of them.

"Hi!" they chorused, standing in a line on the pavement with hands on hips. Rick could not decide if they resembled gunslingers or ballet dancers. They looked ridiculous and threatening at the same time.

"Hi, babe. What brings you to this neck of the woods?" said the tallest.

"On our way back from Baba Jan," Annabel didn't offer any more detail and she didn't introduce Rick.

"Ditto babe, but Katmandu."

There seemed to be a lot of posing and posturing. It was hard to make out which of these laid back pseudo-hippies had had the wildest experience. Rick knew it wasn't him. Annabel seemed calm and aloof. How well she plays the Sphinx, he thought. It was a relief to say goodbye and get going again.

Two hours later they camped up a woodland track in a clearing. Rick collected twigs and firewood. It was all

Road trip Isfahan 1969

rather green and there was not much dried grass or paper; the fire just smoked and smouldered. Annabel decided to help it along by adding a splash of petrol. The result was dramatic: the fire was blown apart and flaming brands were scattered all over the place.

"Christ Annabel, if it wasn't for your glasses you might have lost an eye."

Her face was black like a coal miner and she was so shocked that her normally large blue eyes were the size of saucers. He held her in his arms; she shuddered.

"You look so funny!"

"My shirt is ruined!"

The sides of her mouth went down as if she was going to cry.

"Come on, baby, I'll make you a fondue."

Rick remade the fire and it was soon blazing away. He cut up cheese and heated it over the flames with some milk. Annabel poured out the wine.

"Not bad, babe," said Rick, tasting a mouthful and sipping the wine.

"Don't you babe me." Annabel laughed.

"Next stop Austria," he said.

-§-

They made a detour on country roads that took them up a valley shadowed by tall pine trees, to the Austrian border. The scenery was worth the extra miles. Where a spring gushed out of the hillside, Rick stopped and helped Annabel fill up the water carriers. It was getting cooler and she was wearing her tight blue jeans with the tea-towels sewn into the legs to make flares.

Road trip Isfahan 1969

"Don't look at my bottom like that!"

"Why? Isn't it the most beautiful blue bottom in the world?"

Annabel stood stock still and for a moment Rick thought she was going to pounce on him and roll him in the dirt. He braced himself but she just laughed.

"Don't look so frightened! Just don't think you can ever treat me as a sex object."

"Sex object? What's that?"

-§-

Graz was the first town they came to and compared to what they had become accustomed it seemed so affluent.

"These rows of neat houses look so suburban," commented Annabel. "I am not sure I like it."

After Bruck, the road climbed up through the foothills of the Alps and it grew colder and colder, but the scenery was breath-taking: rivers rushing down through gorges and pine trees climbing steeply up towards snow covered mountain peaks. They pulled off the road and made camp, but up at this altitude it was too cold to sleep and by 2am they were wide awake and shivering. Rick tried to zip their two sleeping bags together to make one big one, but when they tried to climb into it the zip broke. They clung together but it was hopeless.

"It's too cold to make love," said Rick.

"Speak for yourself!"

"I am! Let's get going."

Rick struggled to get free but Annabel clutched him. They wrestled with the bedding and with each other,

Road trip Isfahan 1969

getting quite warm in the process. Rick pulled on his jacket.

"Let's go!"

"Stop! I can't find my specs!"

This was a serious emergency for Annabel. Rick soon found them under the pile of bedding, intact. She kissed him.

Dawn was breaking as they arrived in Salzburg; coffee houses were already opening. They parked outside the Black Cat.

"How do you know it's called the Black Cat?" asked Rick.

Annabel pointed up at the sign.

"Looks like something that should belong to a witch!"

Coffee, black bread, butter and jam was ordered and they sat back thawing out and stretching.

Another border and they were headed for Munich, with its famous sex museum, but they stopped only to buy cold meat, chocolate spread, apples, bread and biscuits, enough for one day.

"Sex museum next?" asked Rick.

"No thank you," answered Annabel.

They joined the autobahn, travelling fast; Nuremburg and then Wurzburg were a distant blur; a landscape of hills and fields divided by woods, rolled by. It was all very lush and green and well-tended after the dust and heat of the Middle East.

The autobahn stretched ahead with no end in sight. Annabel was looking out of the window. "I'm bored," she told Rick. She wriggled round and turned towards

Road trip Isfahan 1969

him. She placed both hands on his thigh and slowly caressed him.

Rick did not take his eyes off the road, but he smiled. "I love you, Annabel."

She unzipped his shorts, loosened his belt and buried her head in his lap.

"Oh! Watch out, we're going to crash!"

Annabel did not stop right away and when she did come up for air she was laughing. Rick had to keep driving but he so wanted to stop and make love to her.

"What shall I do next?" asked Annabel.

They were driving down the middle lane, steadily overtaking a long string of lorries all heading for the border and the coastal ports of Holland. Black Mercedes Benz were overtaking them in the outside lane at about 100mph. Annabel turned and watched the powerful cars racing past. Without warning, she pulled up her T-shirt and exposed her boobs to a passing driver. The Mercedes swerved and narrowly missed the central barrier before careering on faster than ever, but then he seemed to change his mind, pulled over onto the hard shoulder and stopped by a telephone. Rick did not think much of it as they continued sedately on their way, until that is, he saw flashing blue lights coming up behind him. The police car overtook them, slowed down and indicated that they were to pull over and stop. The policeman came over to Annabel's side and motioned to her to wind down the window. He looked at her and she looked innocently back at him. Then realising his mistake, he walked round to the driver's side and spoke to Rick in flawless English. "May I see your papers, please?"

Road trip Isfahan 1969

Rick showed him his driving licence, his international drivers licence, his insurance and his passport, for good measure.

The officer looked at them with a grave expression and then came to the point:

"The driver of a black Mercedes has complained that a young woman flashed him."

"Flashed him, constable? What do you mean?" Rick thought for moment that perhaps the policeman did not know what flashed meant in English. He was soon put right.

"A young woman showed her breasts to a passing motorist. Obviously, a dangerous thing to do on an autobahn."

"And you think it was my little sister here? But she is hardly out of school and would never do such a thing."

"There are not many blue English Land Rovers with white sunroofs in this part of Germany."

Now Annabel felt it was her turn to address the policeman, who had been joined by his colleague.

"I was just very hot and sweaty, constable and I wanted to change my top. I didn't think I was doing anything wrong."

"She is only a child," added Rick.

"Well young lady you certainly have a very small bust," said the copper scrutinising Annabel's slight figure. "Get out of the car, but mind the traffic!"

Annabel did as she was told and the officer walked slowly round her. Rick clenched his teeth, it looked as if the man might be going to ask her to undress, he could feel his pulse starting to race. Annabel gave the fellow a guileless smile. Indeed, she did look just for a moment

Road trip Isfahan 1969

like a dumb blonde. Her eyelashes fluttered over her big blue eyes. The policeman and his mate started to laugh.

"I can't see what all the fuss is about, even if she were to strip stark naked and stand in the middle of the road, she would still be just a child. Take her home to her mother. I am surprised that she let you two out on your own."

His colleague smiled at Rick:

"Your flies are undone, Sir."

The officers got back in their car and roared off.

"Just a child...out on our own…I know I don't have much of a bust, but I'm not completely flat chested, am I?"

"No, not at all. You have the perfect figure. If he had asked you to take off your clothes he would have seen that. But I am very glad he didn't!"

"Stop at the next service station and make love to me," she said as she zipped up his fly. "I need reassurance that I really am as lovely as you pretend."

He did exactly as he was told. Annabel smiled like a tiger and whispered in his ear: "You make me feel just like a woman."

"I love you so much," he said.

He was worried that now she had discovered sex; she would run off with someone else. She seemed to intuitively understand him:

"You don't think I'm a tart, do you? You're the only one I will ever love. Will you love me for ever?"

"Yes, for ever and ever."

"You liar! You're a man, aren't you? Men are never faithful to one woman."

"There have been examples," he said.

Road trip Isfahan 1969

"In history books!" she replied.

The sun was setting as they crossed the Rhine at Cologne, in a lay-by just beyond the bridge was a kiosk selling coffee; they leant against the Land Rover and watched as the red ball of the sun sank behind the spires. Annabel shivered; Rick leant into the back and pulled out a rug to wrap around her shoulders. He stood behind her, holding her in his arms, and sang softly in her ear:

"When summer ends……"

"Even Bob Dylan has a better voice, and anyway you don't have a true love in the north country: I am your first, last and only true love."

"Yes. I didn't realise it at first but you are indeed."

Outside Brussels they stopped one last time for coffee to keep themselves awake. It was like the end was in sight; the church clocks tolled midnight as they arrived in Ostend; Annabel bought a ferry ticket with the last of her travellers' cheques. There was less than an hour to wait before boarding began. They had been on the road since 3.30am.

"You must be exhausted, Rick, I wish I could drive. I am not much use to you, am I?"

"You're all I'll ever want."

On board, they bought some Cherry Brandy from the duty-free shop. Up on deck they swigged it out of the bottle as the ship approached England and dawn made the white cliffs of Dover glow pink and yellow. Standing there at the rail, holding Annabel wrapped in a blanket, rocking gently with the motion of the sea, Rick felt tears welling up; soon he was sobbing uncontrollably. Annabel looked alarmed.

"What is it, lovely?"

Road trip Isfahan 1969

"I was thinking how when we set out from Dover I was so clueless and so anxious. I was remembering how much you impressed me with your flawless French, how cross you got, and how you reduced me to tears at one point. It all seems so long ago now."

"I was the one reduced to tears," she said. "I got you all wrong: I thought you were completely hopeless, and that first night, I did wish that I had never come, in fact I started planning how I was going to get back home."

Rick heaved a sigh and sniffed. "Did you? I never guessed that."

"But I am so glad I stuck it out. When you rescued me from that awful American I realised that you might be alright."

Rick started to shiver, uncontrollably. Annabel made him sit down.

"You're exhausted, lovely. As soon as we get out of Dover we must find a place where you can have a good sleep."

She held him in her arms and rocked him.

"We're home at last, no more worries about food and fuel," he murmured to himself.

"Nearly," she whispered.

By 6.00am they were through customs and on the road to London. They stopped at the first service station for fuel and the full English breakfast. Rick was too tired to eat and fell asleep with his fork halfway to his mouth. Annabel got up and took him by the arm.

"Come on," she said. "You've got to walk."

They swayed across the car park and Rick stood by the Land Rover while she made up a bed in the back. It was hours later he rolled over.

Road trip Isfahan 1969

"Annabel? Annabel where are you?"

Her blonde head emerged from behind the front seats, blue eyes not able to focus Her voice was gruff, "I'm here! How are you feeling now?"

"Fine! Let's go!"

"Sounds like you're back to normal. You gave me a bit of a fright back there. I thought you would never be able to get us home. You went very odd on the ship. Do you remember?"

"Yes, but I'd rather you didn't mention it to anyone."

"Don't be silly lover, it was nothing, you were just tired."

It late afternoon by the time the Land Rover turned into the drive of Walmer House. Annabel knocked on the peeling blue front door. They waited. The sound of a voice calling and another voice answering could vaguely be heard.

"My lazy brother doesn't want to let us in!"

The door opened and Annabel's mother peered at them over her half-moon glasses.

"Oh, it's you," she said, with surprising lack of emotion.

"Yes, Mum, I'm back."

Annabel stepped over the threshold and hugged her mother, planting a kiss on her cheek. The door slammed to. Rick was left standing with a suitcase in one hand and a rucksack in the other wondering what to do. The door opened again and Annabel put her head out.

"Don't stand there! Come in!" She turned to her mother, "You remember Rick. He's driven me all the way back from Isfahan."

Road trip Isfahan 1969

"You must be tired; it's a long way," the eminent professor smiled, as if she had just remembered Rick. "Have a bath and a rest. Supper will be in an hour."

They hauled their things up to the spare bedroom with the faded blue velvet curtains and ran a bath. Annabel swept the cigarette ends into her hand and deposited them in the bin.

"Sorry about that," she smiled. "Mum is a bit eccentric."

She wriggled out of her clothes and lowered herself into the hot water. Rick followed suit; he got the end with the taps. The towels were old and faded and not exactly fresh, but they were too tired to fuss over niceties.

"I think this is my towel," said Annabel, sniffing it before she handed it to Rick and skipped away into the bedroom. They lay under the sheets wrapped in each other's arms.

"Aren't you going to you own bedroom?" he asked.

There was no answer: she was asleep. It seemed only minutes later that they were woken by her brother shouting up the stairs. They dressed in the smart clothes that had been made for them in Isfahan and made an entrance like a Duke and his Duchess. Her brother looked up.

"Where did you get that dress, sis?"

"In Isfahan, Tom. Don't make any hateful comments. I'm too tired to cope with your warped sense of humour just now."

"No, I am impressed: you look great and somehow different. How did it go?"

Road trip Isfahan 1969

"Amazing. I'll tell you one day but now I'm exhausted. I just have to get back to bed, as soon as we've finished supper."

"And what about Rick? He will want to be going home won't he?" asked her mother.

"No Mum, he is coming back to bed with me!"

Rick went red and choked on his soup.

"What's the matter Rick?" asked Tom. "My sister can be an awful tease sometimes as I'm sure you've found out."

"Rick is my boyfriend," Annabel announced.

"How nice," said her mother.

"Wow. I didn't see that coming sis. I had you down as a regular man hater. You never showed any interest in my friends."

"They were your friends, stupid."

"Children, please. Annabel, it has been so peaceful while you've been away."

Annabel got up and leaving her plate half empty flounced out of the room.

"Come on Rick!"

Rick did not know where to look, but he did know he had to obey her. Muttering apologies he hurried after her, and watched mesmerised as her bottom disappeared up the stairs in front of him. Annabel went along the landing and into her room. Rick thought he had better sleep in the guest room and was just slipping through the door when he felt a hand on his collar.

"You're sleeping in my room," she said.

"But what about your mum and Tom?"

"What about them? You never worried about them before. They won't disturb us."

Road trip Isfahan 1969

"Won't they be a bit shocked?"

"No. This is Oxford, not Godalming."

They hurried back to her room and fell onto the bed. He undressed her bit by bit, not that she was wearing much. But the bed was narrow and after falling out twice, they streaked, stark naked, giggling, down the passage to the spare room and jumped into the double bed.

"This is real luxury, like being married," he told her.

It was noon before they surfaced to find the others had gone out; after an enormous fry-up, they set off for the Cherwell Boat House to hire a punt for the day.

"I suppose I better get home and sort things out for London."

"No. Stay one more night."

"Won't your mum think it a bit odd if I don't go home?"

"I'll handle her and Tom."

"And what about your dad?"

"He keeps to his rooms in Balliol; he doesn't live at home anymore. But we pretend he does, because Mum can't admit that her marriage is over."

"That's really sad. I wondered why you never spoke about him. I was afraid he had died or something."

"I still see him a lot, and he helps me with my assignments, even now!"

Rick shipped the pole and sat down beside her, folding her in his arms, letting the punt drift along on the stream.

"But it must still be hard for you."

"Never let me go."

Road trip Isfahan 1969

Chapter Sixteen
A Party in Oxford

Annabel's studies were going well. Rick had passed his exams and was now doing clinical work as a student on the wards, leading up to finals. They met up at weekends in either London or Oxford.

The phone in the corridor was ringing. Rick had been listening out for it and ran to pick up the receiver.

"Hello! Hello!"

"Oh, hello," said Rick.

The voice at the other end sounded anxious.

"Hi Annabel it's me."

"Thank goodness, I was afraid you might be out and I'd have to leave a message."

"Well this time I'm in. I got your postcard so I was expecting your call. What are we going to do this weekend?"

"Come up to Oxford. There's a twenty first birthday party that we've been invited to."

"Oh great. I'll get the 18.35 from Paddington."

"I'll be at home waiting for you. The party isn't until Saturday so we will have Friday night to ourselves."

-§-

Rick was feeling anxious about the party. It was likely that Annabel would be the only person he knew. She on the other hand had many friends in Oxford and had known most of them since primary school.

He rang the bell and waited. Tom answered the door; he did not bother to disguise the fact that he was

Road trip Isfahan 1969

expecting his girlfriend. He just jerked his head in the direction of the stairs. Rick brushed past him and had reached the first tread when Annabel appeared at the top. She launched herself into his arms. Rick staggered backwards and was only saved from a nasty accident by Tom who caught him under the arms and then dumped them both on the floor.

"Watch it!" he snarled.

Annabel took no notice of her brother; her mouth was clamped over Rick's. They lay entwined on the Persian carpet. Then she levered herself off him and taking his hand, ran back upstairs and into her bedroom. He helped her out of her clothes and they slid in between the sheets. After a while she rolled out of bed. "I'm going to run a bath," she said. He followed her and when she slipped into the water he got in behind her.

"Who have you been seeing this week?" she asked, as he soaped her back.

"Nobody, nothing happened. It's boring without you so I just get on with revising for finals."

He got out first, held out a towel for her and wrapping her up, he carried her back to the bedroom.

"How are Jon and Sam getting on?" she asked.

"Well, I did see them briefly because we went to the pub to celebrate Jon getting a place at Berkeley."

"That's exciting, what is he going to do there?"

"A PhD. He will be away for anything up to four years."

"Sam must be quite upset; they've only just got back together again."

"Yes, she was a bit quiet. She didn't get the chance to go and she thinks he'll never come back."

Road trip Isfahan 1969

"And I bet she thinks some American chick will steal him."

When she was dry Annabel sat in front of her mirror in her underwear putting on her make-up. Rick sat on the bed and watched her.

"Pass me my jeans."

She lay on the floor to wriggle into her skin-tight flares.

"Ready now!"

Brown's was busy and they had to queue by the door. Annabel spied Charles sitting at a table with another guy and two girls. She pushed forwards, boldly announcing that they were meeting friends. Charles waved as they approached and stood to give Annabel a kiss on the cheek. Rick hung back, smiling uneasily at these people he had never seen before. He was not introduced.

"Great to see you guys!" said Annabel. "It certainly saved us waiting for ages for a table. Did you sort out the problem with your car Charles?"

"Yep! All ready for tomorrow night,"

He smiled at Annabel in a way Rick did not like. He was distracted by one of the girls.

"You must be Rick. Annabel has told us all about you. In fact, she hardly talks about anything else. I'm Charlotte by the way."

"Hi. I've known Annabel for a while now. We drove out to Persia last summer but I expect you know that."

"Yes, Charles is my brother; he told me all about it. Apparently, you saved Annabel's life."

Rick was surprised. It never occurred to him that anyone would see it that way. It was not reassuring that

Road trip Isfahan 1969

this girl was Charles' sister. He hoped he had a girlfriend.

"This is Maddie, my best friend, and her boyfriend Peter."

Rick felt more uneasy. Annabel and Charles were having a private conversation, which was only broken up by the waitress who had come to take their order.

Annabel was sitting on the bench seat between Charles and Rick, now she turned to Rick and said:

"I was just discussing changing from Greats to Archaeology. Charles says he can help me do that. He is quite influential in the department."

"That would be good, especially as you might be able to transfer to the UCL Institute of Archaeology. It's in Gordon Square, really near Hall."

Annabel narrowed her eyes. "I hadn't thought of that. I can't imagine studying anywhere but Oxford."

"I know Oxford is in your blood, but you'll have to make the break at some point."

"I don't know why; my parents never have."

"Don't keep Annie all to yourself! Come on Annie tell us all about the time you rescued Rick from drowning in the Black Sea," said Charles.

Rick felt a wave of jealousy sweep over him and he had to look away. Annie indeed, he had never heard her called that; it sounded weird in a way he disliked and intimate in a way that made him cross. Charlotte reached across the table and touched his shoulder. She was looking at him as if she understood.

"I was just saying to Maddie how you drove out to Isfahan. Did you encounter any bandits?"

"No." Rick was scarcely polite.

Road trip Isfahan 1969

"But you did save Annabel's life when she was so ill?"

"Yes. I mean no. No, I didn't. I was just there and tried to keep her comfortable while the illness ran its course."

"Annabel sees it rather differently," it was Maddie's turn to butt in. "She seems to think that if it wasn't for you she wouldn't be here now."

"Don't be so modest we know the truth and we know you're lovers!" said Charles.

"Really this is too much!" protested Rick.

Annabel took him firmly by the arm.

"Calm down Rick, nobody is getting at you. They just don't know you. Maddie has invited us to her birthday party."

"Oh, it's your twenty-first! Congratulations! Happy Birthday for tomorrow and all that," he smiled.

"Actually, my birthday's today, the party is tomorrow because some people have a long way to come."

"Well Happy Birthday for today then. I think you three will be the only people I know."

"And me," said Annabel.

"Yes, I haven't forgotten you, my lovely," he gave her a kiss and put his arm around her shoulders.

"We'll look after him, won't we Charlotte?" said Maddie.

The food arrived and Rick ate in silence while the others gossiped about their Oxford friends.

-§-

Road trip Isfahan 1969

Annabel was sitting at her dressing table, "Pass me the red dress."

He held a ball gown out to her.

"Not that one! It's not even red, and we are not going to a ball!"

He handed her a red mini-dress.

"That's better." she said.

She took a pair of stockings out of a drawer and slid them on being careful to get the line straight down the back of her legs and finally attached the tops to her suspender belt. Rick observed the procedure, spellbound.

"Why the stockings? Don't people wear tights these days?"

"Tights lead to all sorts of complications such as thrush and cystitis, and anyway stockings are sexier don't you think? And my legs are horribly pale."

"I do," he said and started to run his hand up the back of her leg.

They were interrupted by a car hooting in the drive. Charles had come to pick them up in his red Alfa Romeo. Rick was envious. The Land Rover had been sold as soon as they got back from Persia.

"Did you come up by train?" asked Charles.

"Yes. There is no point in keeping a car in London."

"Pity, a car can be very useful when you want to get away from it all."

"Sure but as I'm rarely sober after 6 o'clock, I wouldn't be safe to drive!"

"I've never seen you drunk," said Annabel.

Charles drove fast and they soon covered the short distance to Whyteham. The party was being held in the Rectory. Maddie's parents had spared no expense.

Road trip Isfahan 1969

Caterers had been hired to lay on a huge buffet, which included a whole salmon in aspic. Rick had never even seen such a thing; he wondered what it would taste like. There was very finely carved beef, strange vegetables he did not recognise, and to finish off profiteroles and crème brûlée. It was all laid out in a vast dining room whose French windows opened onto a lawn which ended in a ditch or ha-ha, giving the impression that the neighbouring field and the lawn were one uninterrupted space. As it grew dark the band arrived and set up in what had been the children's enormous playroom.

Rick felt out of place. For a start, he was wearing a black velvet suit; the other guests were all casually dressed in jeans, brightly coloured shirts and Afghan or Persian waistcoats. He stuck close to Annabel who seemed to know almost everyone there.

"You can leave your jacket and tie in the bedroom at the top of the stairs," she advised him.

When he came down again she had vanished He looked anxiously around and noticed Charlotte, standing on her own by the table helping herself to pudding. He went over to her. She smiled at him, which was reassuring, even encouraging. She seemed slightly tipsy already.

"I'm glad you're here," he said. He helped himself to crème brûlée.

"Do you like it?" she asked. "I see you're onto your second."

"Yes, delicious. I've never tasted anything like it. How do they make the top so crunchy?"

"With a blow torch." She laughed as if she had made a joke. "Come outside, when the band gets going we can

Road trip Isfahan 1969

dance on the grass," she said, putting her arm through his.

They kicked their shoes off and went out onto the lawn and stood watching the others for a while, finishing the wine in their glasses.

"I'll get you a drink."

"Go and get a bottle," Charlotte suggested.

She knocked back another glass and threw it over her shoulder into the bushes. Rick put his carefully down on a bench.

"Come on I want to dance," she said, and took his hand.

The band had started a quick number that invited a Charleston, followed by a something slow. Rick put his arms round her and they swayed in time to the music. After the third number, they kissed. It was exciting kissing someone new. She tasted different. The dew on the grass cooled their toes. Annabel seemed to have abandoned him and he felt no remorse.

Charlotte put her mouth close to his ear. "Let's go inside, I expect the others are up in the nursery."

"Nursery?" he asked, puzzled.

"It's not the nursery now, of course, but it is still out of bounds to the parents. It's where Maddie and her friends hang out."

They mounted the main stairs, took a corridor towards the back of the house and climbed a narrow staircase to the hideaway. They entered cautiously. There were cushions and mattresses everywhere. Rick had the fleeting impression that the harem at the Topkapi Palace had been invaded by Vandals. Maddie and Peter were entwined in one corner and various couples who Rick

Road trip Isfahan 1969

had never seen before were either smoking, talking or kissing, or doing all three at once. There was a powerful smell of marijuana. Through the haze Rick made out a familiar form; it was Annabel and she was leaning against Charles. He waved and beckoned them over.

"Hi Rick, it's cool man, don't look so tense. The parents never come up here." He handed a fat roll up to his sister who took a deep drag and handed it to Rick who cautiously inhaled.

"Let me show you," said Charlotte.

She took the spliff and put the wet end in his mouth and then very slowly wrapped her lips around the glowing end and gently blew the smoke into his lungs. Rick collapsed backwards in a coughing fit and the others laughed, while he struggled to sit up. Annabel and Charles were totally absorbed in one another. He had his hand on her thigh, when he pushed her onto her back, he was almost on top of her. They started kissing. Rick looked away, confused and anxious, out of his depth in this laid back and promiscuous environment. He felt betrayed but uncertain what to do. Whatever else he must stay cool. He turned back to Charlotte but didn't know what to say. "What are you reading?" he ventured.

"Shush," she said. "Just let your mind float away. Take another drag."

She manoeuvred herself around behind him and kneeling put her hands over his eyes.

"What do you see?" she asked.

Rick could feel her breath on the back of his neck, she was pressing herself against him.

"Stars and more stars and... angels!"

"Keep your eyes shut," she said.

Road trip Isfahan 1969

She put her arms around him, undid the buttons of his shirt and started caressing him. Her hands moved lower. He rolled over, pulled her on top of him, and slid his hands under her mini-skirt.

"I've got to go to the bathroom," she said. "Come with me."

He followed her out into the corridor. As they passed a bedroom, she opened the door and pushed him inside.

"Wait," she commanded. "I'll be back."

He lay on the child's single bed and wondered what would happen next. Charlotte reappeared and tried to lie down beside him, but the bed was too narrow. She knelt and straddled him. It was obvious that she had removed her knickers. She helped him struggle awkwardly out of his trousers.

"Are you safe?" he asked.

"Yes, I am now," she whispered in his ear, and started kissing him; they made love. It seemed she was cut out to be a jockey.

Through the thin walls they could hear another couple in the throes of passion. Charlotte dismounted.

"Let's see who it is!" she laughed.

They tiptoed into the corridor and opened the door of the next room. Charles was in the act of making love to Annabel. She was kneeling on the bed and her dress was around her waist. Rick felt confused and exhausted; confusion gave way to anger. He had wanted Charlotte, no doubt about that but now it felt so wrong. Charlotte dived back into the nursery, Rick excused himself.

"I've got to clear my head."

He made it down the stairs and into the garden. He sat down on the bench where he had left his glass and the

Road trip Isfahan 1969

bottle; to his surprise it was still there, he poured himself a drink in the hope that it would help him calm down. It had the opposite effect. He knew he must get away before he did something violent and stupid or "uncool" as those bastards upstairs would say. He started off without any clear idea as to where he was going. It was a warm night and his eyes soon became accustomed to the gloom; he walked fast in the direction of Oxford, breaking into a jog trot. Gradually his head cleared and a plan formed in his mind. He focused on getting away from Oxford and Annabel, and getting back to London and Hall.

Road trip Isfahan 1969

Chapter Seventeen
Back in London

Weeks passed and although he thought of Annabel everyday he never felt like trying to contact her. She was so obviously part of the Oxford set and he was equally emphatically not. It was total rejection, he felt stupid and humiliated.

Sam contacted him in the third week to suggest the three of them go to the Angel in Islington. It was Sunday lunchtime and the pub was filling up with regulars waiting for the jazz to start. Jon and Rick went to the bar and ordered toasted steak sandwiches and three pints of Adnams. Sam guarded their seats. A trio started to play and at intervals they were joined by friends from the audience who just happened to have their instruments with them. It was totally spontaneous; a group of jazzmen just fooling around. Rick was completely absorbed in the music, oblivious to the other two.

For Sam and Jon, term was coming to an end. For Rick, it meant finals and then a long vacation before starting work. They were going to the USA to check out Berkley, and he was planning to see the States by Greyhound bus.

"Not going on your own, are you?" asked Sam.

"Well I was hoping that Annabel would come with me but now...." his voice trailed off.

Sam put her arms around him.

"Come on. Don't be so negative, you should contact her. Go to Oxford next weekend and have it out with her. I bet she's missing you."

She smiled as if she knew something that he did not.

Road trip Isfahan 1969

As the week went by Rick made a plan. He wrote to Annabel and included a poem that he had written for her after their visit to the Topkapi Palace.

> From the Palace Walls
> A broken pot
> made us dream
> of a lost Bronze Age
> at Baba Jan.
>
> A random collection of jewels, swords
> and gold embroidered garments
> encrusted with gems
> made us dream
> of the long-gone rulers
> of an ancient empire.
>
> A magnificent palace:
> courtyards filled with spreading trees,
> and the fragrance of flowering shrubs.
> Shady rooms in summerhouses
> lined with cool divans
> and couches for a Sultan and his ladies.
> Wide flights of steps lead to
> paved walks on walls overlooking the Bosphorus,
> and the Golden Horn,
> where a fleet rides at anchor.
>
> These memories,
> make me dream of you.

Road trip Isfahan 1969

He looked up the trains to Oxford and then waited for the weekend. The days dragged by and he wished he had decided to leave on Friday night but second thoughts told him that arriving late at night might not be the best way to effect a reconciliation. He gritted his teeth and fretted.

The train rattled through the countryside where hay making was in progress. Rick tried to read but it was difficult to concentrate on Gormenghast, every time Fuchsia was mentioned he saw Annabel's face. It was still only 9 o'clock when he got out of the carriage and he wondered if he was too early. What if Annabel was having a lie-in, even worse what if she was having a lie-in with Charles? What if the reason that she had not answered his letter was because she did not want to see him? He passed the barrier and walked towards the bus stop. A familiar form stepped off the bus and began to run towards the ticket office, he had to step aside to avoid being knocked over.

"Annabel!" he shouted, and ran after her.

She looked around and stopped.

"Rick?"

"Annabel, where are you going?"

"To London, quick, or we'll miss the train!"

She turned and dashed to the window in the ticket hall. Rick followed, wondering why she wanted to go to London in such a hurry.

They sat in window seats with a table between them. He leant forwards and stared at her not knowing what to say. She seemed relaxed now and smiled at him in a way that told him she was back in control. Then, without saying a word she jumped up and came and sat beside

Road trip Isfahan 1969

him, put both arms around his neck and started kissing him. He was in a dream, mouth glued to hers and hands all over her. Luckily the carriage was empty.

"Annabel?"

"Rick?"

"Annabel, I was coming to see you. I hope you got my letter?"

"No, I didn't."

"Then tell me why you are coming to London."

"Dreadful things have happened, Rick. I've been such a fool. I'm sorry if you got hurt."

"But what things Annabel? I thought you had everything sorted."

"I did, Rick, I did. I thought I had the perfect boyfriend; he helped me change courses to Archaeology, I left home and moved in with him."

"Annabel!"

"I'm so sorry, I really am sorry."

She started to cry and he held her, her face pressed against his chest. He stroked her back and murmured in her ear. It was awhile before she looked up.

"Why are you humming in my ear? You haven't changed at all, have you?"

"Oh Annabel, tell me what happened."

"I was so taken in, so betrayed. Charles helped me to change courses only because he wanted to sleep with me, but he didn't really want me, he just wanted a conquest."

"What a bastard, I never felt I could trust him, but when I saw you two together I felt rejected and it looked like you had fallen for him."

"Charlotte was heartbroken when you didn't phone her. She wanted me to give her your number."

Road trip Isfahan 1969

"Why didn't you?"

"Because I felt a bit jealous, and I didn't want her to have you."

"I did kiss her at the party when I saw you and Charles together. But it felt wrong, I was hopelessly confused."

"And the worse for drink and drugs," she reminded him.

"I just had to get away. I felt I had lost you for ever. I just went back to London and concentrated on Finals."

"And I thought you didn't care for me anymore and I was glad because I was so dazzled by Charles. He is the superstar of the department, or so I thought. I didn't realise I could be so naive."

"You're lovely and trusting, not naive. He tricked you just like he tricked people at school."

"Yes. He told me how jealous he had been of you at school."

"Poor Annabel, but why did you split up, you still haven't told me."

"I went to his flat last Thursday. I had been working late at home all week, because we have exams soon and all the things I need are still there. I often fell asleep in my own bed. Then that evening I thought I mustn't neglect my new boyfriend, so I stole a bottle from the cellar and went around to his place to surprise him."

"Bad move I should think," said Rick.

"It was indeed. He was there, but so was Maddie. They did look a bit sheepish, and when I went to the loo I noticed the bed looked as if it hadn't been made. Men, I thought, so untidy. Then I saw Maddie's knickers on the

Road trip Isfahan 1969

floor. I felt sick, I ran into the bathroom and vomited in the basin."

"How did you know they were Maddie's?"

"That's irrelevant, Rick. They were hers alright. She's half French and does all her shopping in Paris."

"I never knew that."

"Rick be serious, this is important to me. I made some feeble excuse and ran all the way home."

"But that was all a week ago, why didn't you contact me?"

"Because trying to ring your Hall is hopeless, I wrote you a letter, didn't you get it?"

"No. But why are you on this train now?"

"I am going to look around the Institute of Archaeology and have an informal interview. There now you know."

"I'm a bit confused, how did you get the introduction to the Institute?"

"Through Sam, of course. I had to tell her why I wanted to get out of Oxford so badly and she told me how sad you were feeling."

"So you thought you would kill two birds with one stone?"

"No Rick, I wasn't sure you would want me back, so I was still debating if I would come round to Hall after the interview or not."

"Of course I want you back, I don't want to let you out of my sight ever again."

-§-

Road trip Isfahan 1969

When Rick got back to Hall Annabel's letter was in his pigeonhole. He sat on his bed wondering what it said; cautiously he slit the envelope. It opened with a poem:

>From the Seraglio
>To a wild hawk
>
>I am trapped here gazing out over the Bosphorus,
>From paved walks on castle walls.
>You are free.
>In my dreams
>I hear you calling to me,
>from the snow-capped mountains,
>and dusty plains of Asia,
>which were my home too.
>Why have you come to disturb me?

She had crossed out the last line and written in her clear neat hand: Will you forgive me? Then: I've made a big mistake but I'm determined to put it right. I will be in London on Saturday, can I come and visit you?

LOVE Annabel (Tiger) XOXOXO

Rick read the lines over and over again. He had never thought that Annabel would admit she could make a mistake and despite what she had already told him on the train, it made him smile. She meant what she had said: here it was in writing, in her own hand.

Annabel walked in without knocking, just like in the old days.

"Hi, how did you get on?"

"They offered me a place. I start in the autumn and I don't have to repeat the first year."

Road trip Isfahan 1969

She smiled her feline smile and stretched out her arms to him. He pulled her down, and rolled on top of her.

"Why did you send that poem?"

"Because I felt trapped in Oxford, Charles was using me, parading me like I was a trophy or something. What made it so bad was that all my friends and even my mother and my hateful brother approved."

She stopped and glared at him; squeezed him so hard he could not breathe.

"I am here now and I don't want to think about it, or you to mention it ever again."

He stopped any further conversation with kisses that moved from her mouth down her body, as he undressed her bit by bit. By the time he got to her toes she was stark naked and giggling. She sat up.

"Now it's my turn! Where are the balloons?"

-§-

They made for the Lamb in Lambs Conduit Street. Over beer and scampi in the basket, they made plans.

"Can you come to the USA with me?" he asked.

"I'll book a flight through BUNAC[3], and I expect they will have suggestions for a holiday job."

"Book the flight ASAP, but no need to worry about a job. My cousin will find something for you when we get to Maine."

Road trip Isfahan 1969

Chapter Eighteen
Summertime in the USA

Snow covered peaks and surf breaking on black crags, appeared through a break in the clouds.

"Look Rick," said Annabel.

He leaned over her to get a better view, her scent distracted him for a moment; he could see icebergs and then the rocks.

"What's that down there? I thought we were flying over the Atlantic."

"Greenland, planes take the great circle route, you know."

"I am so glad you're with me, Annabel."

They settled back in their seats to watch Donald Sutherland and Jane Fonda in Klute.

-§-

The queue at passport control moved slowly.

"Don't tell them you're a communist," whispered Annabel.

"Why not?" he whispered back.

"McCarthy."

Rick looked puzzled but there was no time to ask what she meant, they were at the head of the line and she stepped forward to answer seemingly endless questions about the purpose of her visit. He repeated her answers word for word to the same customs officer, as she disappeared in the direction of the baggage hall.

Road trip Isfahan 1969

-§-

BUNAC had arranged for them to spend the first two nights in a downtown YMCA Hostel in Greenwich Village.

"I'll take you to The Slide," said Rick.

"What's that?"

"It was one of the most notorious speakeasies in the time of prohibition, but now it is a respectable restaurant."

They wandered down the street passing brownstone buildings with their iron fire escapes, they crossed Washington Square, and entered Little Italy. They couldn't find the restaurant that Rick had in mind so they settled for the Millie Pini.

"You are mad, you know that Rick?"

"Why do you say that, Honey?"

"Taking me out to dinner, like I'm a Southern Belle."

"Why not, Honey?"

"Because we have no money and stop calling me Honey, people here might think you are taking the piss, even I'm not quite sure!"

The waiter came over and smiled at Annabel. She ordered seafood linguine and he ordered tournedos Rossini, and a bottle of Chianti.

"We'll swap over if you like, this is just delicious," he said.

"Just cut me off a bit," she said, heaping a spoonful of linguine onto his plate.

He cut off a bit of steak and held it out to her on his fork.

"Shut your eyes and open your mouth."

Road trip Isfahan 1969

"Don't be so rude Rick, just put it on my plate."

-§-

From the windows of the Greyhound bus the view of suburban houses set back in their own gardens gave way to pine trees and the rugged coast of Maine. Rick's cousin lived outside Rockport. He was waiting at the bus station to welcome them. Francis owned a café and art gallery on Main Street, but the house was out in the countryside. It was a typical New England homestead clad in pale blue clapboard. They went through into the sitting room.

"Wow," said Annabel

The view from the French windows opening onto the veranda looked out over Penobscot Bay. The dark pine trees came down to the water's edge or in other places overhung towering black crags. At the bottom of the garden was a speed boat moored to a pontoon.

"Can we swim off the jetty?" asked Rick.

Francis laughed.

"You can, but it's bloody cold. The Labrador current runs down this coast from the Artic."

"Who owns the boat?" asked Annabel.

"I do. I'll take you water-skiing once the outboard has been fixed. You'll need wetsuits, but we have plenty of those if you don't mind sharing."

"Hi you guys!" Veronica called out as she entered the house.

They turned round to see a dark-haired woman of about forty enter the room, she was loaded down with

Road trip Isfahan 1969

bags which threatened to spill bread, fruit and bottles of wine.

"Sorry I wasn't here to greet you, but my lazy husband lets me do all the shopping,"

He hurried over to take the stuff from her and as he did so leant forwards for a kiss.

"We won't eat in tonight, kids. For a treat, we are going to Salty's for lobster Américaine."

Francis showed his guests to their room.

"I've given you the double bed. I guess you'll tell me if I've blundered?"

He looked at Annabel. Without blinking she answered:

"I most certainly would, but I'm cool sharing a bed with Rick."

Francis laughed.

"You're picking up the language fast! Have a shower with your steady and we'll get going once you're done! No hurry."

The shower was like nothing they had seen before. An enormous rose poured water down on their heads while multiple jets blasted them from every angle. The shower cubicle was easily big enough for two. Rick soaped her back and bottom. He wanted to make love.

"Not now, Rick. Quit fooling around will ya?"

-§-

They piled into the Lincoln Continental and motored north towards Camden. Salty's was a wooden shack built on piles over the water. It was a warm evening so they sat out on the deck. The light westerly breeze was dying;

Road trip Isfahan 1969

ripples on the water reflected the evening light. Racing yachts with spinnakers set were heading for port.

"They look just like Folkboats," said Rick.

"That's what they are," replied Francis. "One of our millionaire neighbours went over to Europe and brought back a dozen so that he and his friends could race together on Wednesday nights."

"John sold them on to his friends, so it was not an entirely altruistic gesture," said Veronica.

"Did you buy one?" asked Annabel.

"He sure did. It's his pride and joy," said Veronica.

"She. Boats are she," John said.

Veronica laughed. "See how touchy he is when it comes to Bella!"

"Bella's a nice name," said Annabel.

"He made it up out of the names of our daughters: Belinda and Layla."

"That's just lovely," said Annabel.

"Next Wednesday I'll take you both out," John offered.

"That will be great, thank you," said Rick.

"Will you be coming Veronica?" asked Annabel.

"Maybe, it depends. I'm a fair-weather sailor."

"Me too," said Annabel. "In fact I'm not really a sailor at all, but Rick has sailed all his life."

"In dinghies, I don't know about big boats."

"There's no difference, Rick. These Folkboats handle like a dinghy."

-§-

Road trip Isfahan 1969

Next morning Francis took them to the café and put them to work. The place had been a warehouse in the days when all goods came to Rockport by sea; fish and furs had been stored in the warehouse until they could be exported. Now huge picture windows opened on dramatic views of the harbour and in the distance, the islands across the bay. At the far end tables and chairs were arranged to take advantage of the scenery and a bar and food counter ran part of the way along one wall. To get to the seating area patrons had to pass through the gallery where there was an exhibition of paintings by local artists. In the middle of the space was a huge sculpture spelling out the word LOVE.

"Robert Indiana gave us that piece last year, when we had a party to mark our tenth anniversary," said Francis.

"Wow!" said Annabel and moved closer to inspect the large rusty letters, piled up to make a square: LO on top VE underneath.

"Your job, Annabel, is to show people around and answer questions if they show any interest in the pictures," said Francis.

"What is Rick going to do?"

"He's going to make coffee, serve food and wash up. You can ask him to help you when it comes to changing the exhibition."

"Have you ever made a proper cup of coffee, Rick?" she asked.

"I'm good at instant," he replied.

"I may have to help you. Coffee machines can be tricky if you haven't used one before." she said.

Road trip Isfahan 1969

"I'll show him what to do," said Francis. "First let me introduce you both to the pictures: this one is by Jamie Wyeth."

He pointed to a landscape depicting a blue clapboard house on a lonely promontory.

"That could almost be your house," said Annabel.

"Almost," said Francis. "Both Robert and Jamie spend their summers up here."

They continued the tour; Annabel started taking notes but Francis stopped her.

"We've a printed leaflet you can refer to," he told her. "One of your jobs will be updating it from time to time."

They moved to the back of the building. The coffee machine was not so terribly complicated. Francis went off to a meeting in town and left them to it. It wasn't long before they had their first customers. She sat at a table in the window and her partner came over and ordered:

"Pastrami on rye and a Bud for me, coffee and a bagel for my wife."

Rick looked at the man in alarm, what on earth was he talking about? He looked anxiously in the various glass fronted cabinets and spied a can of Budweiser. He poured it into a glass and it frothed everywhere. He opened another can.

"I'll only charge you for one," he said, hoping that Budweiser was indeed what the man wanted. Annabel came to the rescue.

"How does your wife take her coffee?" she smiled.

"Black with hot milk."

"I'll bring it right over," she said.

Road trip Isfahan 1969

When she returned, Rick was still wondering what rye was.

"It's a sandwich on black bread, dummy."

Annabel laughed and went back to the table with the rest of the order.

"Where are you folks from?" asked the wife.

"Oxford, England," said Annabel and beamed at her.

"I just love your accent. Are you going to stay around for the summer?"

"Well yes, for a month or two."

"Well I'm Laura, that's L A U R A and this is Ernest, that's E R N E S T. We come here a lot so I'm sure we will be getting to know you two. Is that your boyfriend over there?"

"Yes he's Rick and I'm Annabel."

She resisted the temptation to spell out their names, as she told Rick later.

"You're cute Honey and so is your man."

Annabel smiled and almost curtsied.

"Have they paid?" she whispered.

"No! I forgot to ask!"

"Never mind I am sure they will on the way out. If not, I'll remind them. What is the bill by the way?"

"I've no idea."

Annabel quickly found a price list and wrote it all down on the waitress's pad.

"Thank God you're here, Annabel. I wish he had asked me to do the pictures and you to do the bar."

"We can swap around from time to time and I'll give you a hand when you get stuck," she laughed.

-§-

Road trip Isfahan 1969

"You got a driving licence, Rick?" Veronica asked.

"Yes."

"Good, you can take Annabel to the pictures in the Lincoln, and we will go along in the pickup. It's no good trying to see a drive-in movie from the back seat."

"Although I notice that some of the high school kids do just that," said Francis.

"He is just being rude and suggestive, take no notice," said his wife, smiling at Annabel.

"OK kids, let's go! First stop McDonalds. I'll lead the way."

Francis climbed into the pickup and turned into the road. Rick and Annabel followed along behind. The pick-up turned into the drive-through take away. Rick saw Francis lean out of the car and talk to the girl in the window.

"What do you want?" he asked Annabel.

"Big Mac, fries and a Coke."

"What's that?"

"Just ask for two and you'll find out!"

"How do you know so much about America?"

"We came on holiday every year for a while. At the time my father was being invited to lecture at different universities and that paid for our trips."

"Gosh, I never realised he was so famous, you never said."

"He isn't, well except in his own very small field."

"What's that?"

"Ancient Roman love poems."

"Catullus?"

"Yes! You're a marvel."

Road trip Isfahan 1969

"Don't be cruel, Annabel. Where did you stay?"
"With his academic friends."
"And did you have an American boyfriend?"
"No my jealous lover, I was only twelve."

The film started. It was cosy sitting in the car finishing the last of the French fries and sipping Coke. Rick was fascinated to note that the car had special places to put the cans, but it was awkward holding hands, eating and drinking all at the same time. The film was To Have and have Not. Slim (Lauren Bacall) was standing outside her hotel room, saying to Morgan (Humphrey Bogart) You know how to whistle, don't you, Steve? Just put your lips together - and blow. Rick abandoned the chips and tried to kiss Annabel.

"Get off me," she hissed. "You don't know how to whistle!"

He whistled.

"Now you're spoiling the film. Sit still and I'll deal with you when we get back to the ranch."

-§-

Rick was amazed how easy it was to drive the big Lincoln. Automatics were a novelty as was the huge engine and the air-conditioning. Fuel seemed ridiculously cheap. Francis let them use the car whenever they wanted. They got into the way of cruising up and down Main Street like real American students. First they would go to the drugstore and buy a six-pack of Schlitz, the beer that made Milwaukee famous.

Road trip Isfahan 1969

"Keep it in the paper bag," advised the shopkeeper. "It's illegal to have any opened bottles or cans of alcohol in a car."

They drove down Main Street. A red E-type Jaguar came towards them, they slowed down. The Jag stopped.

"Hi, you must be the guys from England. My parents told me about you; said you were staying with Francis and Veronica."

"Your parents must be Laura and Ernest. We are getting to know them quite well."

"Yes, they have shares in the café. Would you like to follow us down to the lake?"

The lake was a regular meeting place for students. The water was warm enough for skinny dipping. They sat on the rocks listening to the clinking of beer cans that had been thrown into the water.

"Did you go to Woodstock?" asked Annabel.

She was talking to Jenny whose long dark hair was held back by a headband.

"Yeah, it was just so cool. Where were you in August 1969?"

"Rick was looking after me in a house in Kermanshah, Persia. I was really ill."

"Persia? Wow! What was the matter with you?"

"I had typhoid fever."

"I guess you were lucky to survive. At least no-one at Woodstock died of typhoid."

"Did you get to hear Janice Joplin?"

"Yeah, but it was 3am. I was drunk, she was stoned and I can't remember any of it."

"There's a great recording. I love Ball and Chain."

Road trip Isfahan 1969

Lawrence, owner of the Jag, was on leave from the army. He'd done a tour in Vietnam.

"I don't like to talk about it all that much," he said and changing the subject, he turned to Annabel.

"Let me take you for a ride in the Jag."

"Only if Rick can come too," she answered.

The three of them piled into the car and roared off into the night.

"This is such a great car. I love these English motors, although the engine is tiny, the road holding is great."

"Tiny compared to the Lincoln," said Rick. "In England 4.2 litres is regarded as large."

"That's what I mean; the Lincoln is 7.5 litres."

The Jag went into a four-wheel slide round the next bend.

"Stop!" screamed Annabel. "You'll kill us all."

"But what a way to die, eh chick? Better than napalm!"

Annabel went white but they got back to the lake in one piece. Lawrence wandered over to his buddies.

"Take me back to the house, Rick. These guys are mad."

-§-

It was time to change the exhibition. Francis planned to show local artists for two weeks. He closed the café for the day; Rick took down pictures while Francis and Annabel selected new ones to put in their place.

"It's great having you here, I miss Belinda when it comes to this sort of stuff."

"Where is Belinda now?"

Road trip Isfahan 1969

"She has moved out to the coast. She's at Berkeley."

"Won't she come home for the holidays?"

"No, she has a job, she's got to work her way through college, but she'll be home for Thanksgiving."

Pictures were propped up all around the walls. Rick was sweeping the floor when Veronica walked in.

"No, No, No, you can't hang those two together!" she exclaimed.

Francis looked at Annabel and laughed.

"Don't be offended, Veronica always says that."

"And I'm always right! You have to stand up to him Annabel, he has no idea."

Annabel smiled and moved the pictures around, ready for Rick to start hanging.

"That's better. Rick, help me get the food out of the car. The cases of wine are really heavy."

"Food?" asked Rick.

"Yes, food and drink! Didn't Francis tell you we are having a vernissage this evening. Really! He's hopeless. Still he's a man and all men are useless. I expect you're the same, I'll have to keep a close eye on you."

They sat in the café area to eat lunch. Out on the water the sun was sparkling and a large yacht was beating up towards Camden.

"That's Anjaca, her owner is the guy who bought all those Folkboats," said Francis.

"Boys, forget boats for a moment and let me fill you in on my plans for this evening," said Veronica.

The afternoon was spent setting up tables and putting the sandwiches and vol-au-vents out under plastic wraps.

"I want to buy something to wear for this evening, Rick," said Annabel.

Road trip Isfahan 1969

"A frock?"

"Maybe, can you drive me into town in a minute?

They parked on Main Street and went shopping.

"I had no idea clothes would be so cheap," said Rick. "I'll get some jeans and a t-shirt and look like a smart college student!"

"Did you know that college students have to work in the holidays to pay for tuition fees?"

"No, what an extraordinary idea," said Rick.

Annabel bought a cotton print dress and a pair of shorts with a flap across the front so that they looked like a skirt from in front and shorts from behind.

"That's too weird, Annabel, even a bit coy."

"But very American, Rick. I've seen lots of girls wearing them."

-§-

"You two stand by the door and welcome guests with tickets and keep the riffraff out. When most people have arrived, I want Annabel to help me supervise the food, i.e. stop Francis eating it all," Veronica laughed.

"What shall I do?" asked Rick.

"When a painting has been bought, I'll give you a red sticky dot to put in one corner."

Annabel and Rick conscientiously scrutinised each ticket; the gallery was filling up when a tall dark haired man with black rimmed spectacles walked up to the door and stepping round Annabel joined the crowd.

"Hey, you can't just walk in here," she said, staring up at him with her large blue eyes.

"Why not Honey?" he asked with a smile.

Road trip Isfahan 1969

"You need a ticket."

"Show me that programme you're holding."

She held it out and he pointed to a line which read: Gordon will be joining us to sing sea chanties.

"Are you Gordon?"

"Yep, and I'd be much obliged if you'd show me where to set up the lights and the mikes for the show."

"I'll get Francis."

Annabel retreated into the crowd, leaving Rick to help Gordon.

"Where are your things?" he asked.

Gordon smiled.

"My guitar is in the car."

"He doesn't need a mike or lights! He's teasing you," said Francis when she found him. "He can sit on a chair and strum his instrument like the old salt he pretends to be."

Gordon was standing behind him; Annabel made a gesture to warn Francis; he turned around and the two men hugged, and laughed like old friends.

Most of the guests had left by the time Gordon got around to tuning his twelve-string guitar and settled himself on a stool by the picture window. It was growing dark and the last of the evening light sent silky reflections across the water behind him. He played a chord and started.

"Away to the west, a place a man must go," or something like that.

People stopped talking and gathered round. He had a deep baritone voice; as Rick listened he realised that the song was about Brittany. Then there was a song from Liverpool, before he came back to the Bay of Fundy.

Road trip Isfahan 1969

The weather was bad and the sailors were worse; cruelly deserting their wives and sweethearts, who were not that faithful it seemed. Rick and Annabel sat side by side sipping their wine, spellbound.

-§-

On Wednesday, they closed the café early and drove over to Camden to join Francis on Bella. It was a lovely clear evening with a light breeze from the west. Veronica was kneeling on the foredeck packing the spinnaker.

"Hi Annabel, we'll work together. I'll look after you."

Francis grinned at Rick.

"Veronica is a great bowman and much lighter than most blokes, an advantage on a small boat like this. I want you to helm while I do tactics and main sheet. The girls will trim the genny."

"Thank you!"

Rick felt quite apprehensive, but the system worked well. With Francis standing in the middle of the boat, keeping an eye on the opposition and the wind shifts, the other members of the crew could concentrate on their jobs knowing that he would be instantly available should they need help. They reached along the line, then did a timed run.

"OK, dump everything,"

"What does that mean," Annabel asked.

"Just let the sheets go so that the sails flap."

"Sheets are the ropes holding the sails in, right?"

"Yep."

Road trip Isfahan 1969

The boat slowed and they waited as Francis counted down to the start. With perfect timing, he called: "Sheet in, we're racing, don't pinch Rick,"

They went for the middle of the line and crossed as the gun went. To windward a luffing match was taking place, allowing Bella to sail through their lee and climb towards the top mark. Francis was talking to Veronica.

"Get ready for a starboard pole."

She handed the genny sheet to Annabel.

"Hold this while I get the spinnaker ready, Francis will tell you what to do."

She moved onto to the foredeck. Francis loosened the starboard sheets and guys, indicating to Annabel to do the same on the other side. Veronica moved the sail bag onto the port side and attached the halyard. As they bore away round the top mark, Francis put a turn round the winch with the spinnaker halyard and handed it to Annabel:

"Tail that," he told her.

Annabel looked at Rick.

"He means pull it," he whispered.

Veronica, up at the mast, went for the hoist; Annabel pulled like mad, Francis set the guy and trimmed the sheet. They accelerated past a boat that seemed to be having problems: their spinnaker was wrapped around the forestay. Rick's only job was to keep the boat sailing fast. Francis decided in which direction. They moved out to the starboard side of the course and prepared to gybe. Veronica stood with her back to the mast; Francis took the sheet in one hand and the guy in the other.

"When I give you the guy, put on another turn and cleat it off," he told Annabel.

Road trip Isfahan 1969

"Run dead downwind now, Rick," he said.

Veronica unclipped the pole from the mast and attached it to the port clew. She clipped the free end back on the mast.

"Come up, slowly now!" said the skipper. "Hey! Great job, boys!"

Rick altered course and they were heading straight for the bottom mark. Veronica joined them in the cockpit.

"Why didn't we just sail directly to the mark?" Annabel asked her. "And why does he call us boys?"

She said it so quietly that Francis who was just concentrating on his next move did not hear her.

Veronica laughed: "It's never fast to run dead down wind, so we always put in an extra gybe."

"And we will be ready for the next beat and won't have to gybe at the mark, while jockeying for position with the other boats," said Rick.

"What are you girls wittering about?" called Francis.

"Now Rick's an honorary girl. That's for talking when you should be concentrating Rick!"

"Guys! Guys! We're racing!" called the boss, but still in a good humour.

It seemed they must get to the mark with a good lead. It was time to drop the spinnaker. Veronica went forward to trip the guy. Francis told Annabel just how far to let the halyard go and got ready to pull the sail into the cockpit with the sheet. They started to come up, the boat healed. Veronica reached up and tripped the guy, lost her footing and fell into the water, just as they passed the mark. Rick spun the boat head to wind and she stopped, sails flapping. Francis grabbed the heaving line and

Road trip Isfahan 1969

swinging it round, sent it flying towards Veronica who was swimming after them like she was going for Olympic gold. She grabbed it; he pulled her to gunwale and heaved her back into the cockpit.

"Bear away!" he shouted.

It was the first time he had raised his voice that afternoon.

"Pull that sheet to back the jib, Annabel," said Rick putting the helm up.

Bella payed off and gathered speed. Veronica went below and started to strip off her wet clothes.

"You alright 'Nica?" Francis called down the companionway. "Want me to come below and share some bodily warmth?"

"Keep your dirty thoughts to yourself," she shouted back.

She was up in the cockpit in minutes, in dry clothes. Then began a desperate tacking battle up the shore out of the tide. Veronica worked one winch and Annabel the other; they were soon glowing. Francis appeared to take no notice. He stayed in the middle of the boat watching the opposition and calling the tacks. Rick just kept the sails full and the boat sailing high and fast. A cannon boomed out its message. Francis turned to Veronica; putting his arms around her he lifted her off her feet.

"Done it again girl!"

"Did we win?" asked Annabel.

"We sure did!"

They dropped sails and started the old outboard to motor into the harbour and moor up by the yacht club. At the bar Rick tried to buy the drinks, but Francis insisted. Veronica came back from the notice board.

Road trip Isfahan 1969

"We're winning the series," she announced.

Ernest came up behind Francis and clapped him on the back so that his beer went down his front. "Lost a man overboard and still took line honours! I don't believe it. Is there no stopping you?"

"I'm surprised he went back for you Veronica!" said Laura.

"He didn't. I had to swim after them!"

"The only reason he picked you up is because it's against the rules to finish a race with less crew that you start with," said Ernest.

Annabel and Rick watched the old friends with open eyes.

"Actually, we won because of my blue-eyed girl here, worth two of your boys Ernest!"

"And what about her lover?" asked Veronica.

"Oh he's OK, as helms go."

"Ignore him Rick. You're the best helm we've had on the boat in quite a while. If you hadn't stopped so quickly I would still be out there swimming!"

"Yes," said Francis. "I was only pulling your leg. Now that I've seen how you handle a boat I'm happy for you and Annabel to take Bella out anytime you want."

"We could go camping on one of the islands," said Rick as they snuggled up in bed together after a merry evening at the club.

-§-

It was time to go back home to London, England. On their last evening, they took the Lincoln up to the Lookout, a hill above Camden. They parked the car off

Road trip Isfahan 1969

the road by a gate into a field and climbed the last two hundred yards to the top. The Lookout was a brick built, two roomed cottage that had been occupied by the coastguard in years gone by. Now it was empty and kids used it as a trysting place.

"I don't want to go home," said Annabel. "I just want to stay here with you."

"We'd get very hungry, up here on our own."

"People would bring us food; the raven might drop us a crust."

"The only thing Lawrence would bring us is dope."

They laughed, remembering the first time they had come up here with Lawrence and his friends. The sun was setting behind the pine clad mountains of New England; a silky sheen coloured the waves between Camden and the islands in the far distance. Rick put his arm around Annabel and kissed her, slowly at first, then more passionately. He slid his hand under her t-shirt. She stopped kissing:

"Don't Rick we can't do it here."

"Yes we can," he whispered in her ear and outlined a plan that made her giggle.

Dusk was turning to dark when they regained the road. To Rick's alarm a policeman complete with gun was standing by the car.

"What ya doin' up there?"

He sounded aggressive; he clearly suspected they were up to no good.

"We've just been watching the sunset from the Lookout, officer," said Annabel. "We didn't do any damage or anything."

"But you are trespassing."

Road trip Isfahan 1969

"I'm really sorry, officer," said Rick.

"Your accents just crack me up! Get out o' here and don't come back!"

Chapter Nineteen
The Wedding
1979

Their student days were over. Rick and Annabel wandered down Kensington Church Street, turned left past the antiques market and went into Kensington Gardens. They stood on the edge of the Round Pond, watching the model yachts.

"Camden and Rockport seem so far away," said Annabel.

Rick looked at her in her short summer dress: her arms were clasped across her front, she was shivering. He hugged her and kissed the top of her head.

"You sound sad," he said. "Let's go and get some crumpets for tea and a sweater for you from M&S."

She tilted her head back and kissed him. "I love you," she said.

-§-

They took their crumpets and tea to bed and cuddled up.

"It would be nice to have a log fire in the winter," she said.

"It would be nice to have our own place!" he replied.

"We should get married."

She peered at him in her short-sighted way to see what affect her words had. He gazed at her large blue eyes and pulled her down for a kiss.

"I never thought you'd ask," he said.

"Now ask me," she said.

Road trip Isfahan 1969

Rick wriggled out from under her and kneeling on the bed, holding her head in his hands, said:

"Please marry me Annabel. I promise to make you happy."

Taking a paperclip, he bent it into a ring and pushed it on her finger. She took it off and threw it in the wastepaper basket under his desk.

"I'll say yes if you get me the real thing."

He pushed her over and started to undress her. She pulled his shirt off over his head and started on his jeans.

"Kneel," he whispered in her ear, when they were both naked.

"Lie down," she commanded.

He lay down on his stomach.

"Don't be so cussed awkward," she said. "Turn over."

He turned over; she crawled across the bed and pounced on him like a tiger.

-§-

He bought a diamond ring from a friend in the antiques market on the High Street. Clarence was a somewhat dubious character but he solemnly promised it was the real thing.

Rick took Annabel out to dinner and hid the ring in her pudding. At the last minute, he panicked at the thought that she might swallow it and choke to death:

"Stop! Don't eat that."

Annabel had the spoon halfway to her wide-open mouth. She shut it and looked up.

Road trip Isfahan 1969

"What? Why ever not? Death by chocolate is my favourite."

"Yes but there is something in it."

She stirred the black stuff round and there was a clink as her spoon hit something hard. She dug a bit more and pulled out the ring.

"Waiter!"

"Madam?"

"There is a ring in my pudding!"

The waiter was about to whisk the dish away. Rick deftly grabbed the spoon and put the ring in his mouth, spat it discreetly into his wine, recovered it and holding it out to Annabel, fell onto his knees:

"Annabel, Sweet Plumb, marry me!"

"Sweet plumb!" she almost shouted. "Never call me that!"

"OK. Tiger, please, please marry me."

The other diners and the waiters and the waitresses were on their feet:

"Yes, say yes," they pleaded.

It was pandemonium.

"YES!" she yelled above the din.

-§-

"Show us, go on, please."

Annabel's fellow teachers at the Primary School in South Kensington crowded round her, all eager to see the ring.

"What does he do, your man?" asked the new teacher.

Road trip Isfahan 1969

"He does all the right things, doesn't he?" said Georgia.

They had started together at the school on the same day.

"Don't be smutty, George. As you know he is an ENT surgeon at the South Bank."

"In training, Annabel. He's not the boss yet."

"No, George, but he soon will be."

"Where are you going to live?" asked Diana.

"Well, we'll stay in the grotty flat with Fred for the moment, but we are thinking of moving south of the river."

"Not Clapham!"

"Why not Clapham? You're a snob, George."

"Because my loathsome brother lives there."

"It's up and coming that is why everyone in moving to Battersea or Cla'ham."

"Wish I had somewhere to live," said Diana.

"But not south of the river. Go north young woman!"

"We would look in Kentish Town or Islington but it's not convenient for Rick."

"Camberwell became a bower, Clapham an Arcadian vale," sang Georgia dancing around the room.

"Peckham! Not Clapham and stop teasing me."

"Where are you living now?" asked Diana.

"In a ground floor flat in Kensington Church Street, we share with Fred, one of Rick's friends from school."

"That sounds terribly grand."

"Sadly it isn't. We have our double bed in the front room and Fred has his in the back room, which is also the dining room. Kitchen and shower are all in one room out the back."

"You're real slum dwellers," said Georgia. "But I tell you what."

"What?" said Annabel, dreading what she would come up with next.

"When you've gone, Diana could move in with Fred. They are so suited to each other."

"Rubbish. Don't listen to her Diana. She is just being silly."

"But I would have one room and he would have the other, we wouldn't have to sleep together," said Diana.

"Ho-ho, you don't know Fred!" said Georgia.

"Stop it George. You don't know Fred at all; he has a very nice girlfriend down in Guildford," said Annabel.

"What are we going to call you?" asked Diana.

"Mrs Griffin!" said Annabel.

-§-

That weekend they drove down to Oxford in Annabel's Mini and stayed at Walmer House. Over baked jacket potatoes and cold meat, Annabel announced their engagement. Her mother looked dubious. Tom was not pleased. Next day when they ran her father to earth at his rooms in Balliol, he was delighted.

"I feared she would marry an academic and spend the rest of her life in Oxford," he told Rick. The three of them went off to the Turf to celebrate.

-§-

Road trip Isfahan 1969

Choosing a wedding dress was easy. Annabel bought a short, white transparent number with small red roses from a charity shop.

Her mother, however, had different ideas and in the end a compromise was reached. Rick looked on in amazement while the two women went from shop to shop trying on long, short, flowery, flouncy, lacy, white and cream dresses. In the end the short white transparent dress was thrown out in favour of a simple cream creation in silk with a short train. Rick didn't know Elizabeth very well but had assumed she was a rational person, now mother and daughter were communicating on a level way beyond anything he could imagine and it seemed to be making them happy.

"Why not red?" Rick asked. "In India the bride always wears red."

"Eh? Perhaps because I'm not getting married in India."

Rick whispered something in her ear and Annabel replied, making sure everyone in the shop could hear:

"You're not a virgin either, but I don't expect you to wear a red badge on your morning coat."

Elizabeth stopped talking to the florist and turned just in time to see her daughter slap her future son-in-law.

"Don't you mean scarlet letter, darling?" she asked. "What do you think of a bouquet of red roses?"

"Lovely," said Annabel.

"Great," said Rick.

"That's decided then," said a triumphant Elizabeth.

-§-

Road trip Isfahan 1969

Only immediate family were invited.

"Why all the secrecy? Why no guests and no party?" asked Tom. "Are you pregnant?"

"No, I'm not!" said Annabel. "I just don't want a big ostentatious wedding. It's just about me and Rick. It would have been in the registry office, except that Mum insists that we go to the chapel and Dad gives me away."

In due course, it turned out that loads of people had to be invited. Not only relations but also old friends and even Charles, Charlotte, Maddie and Peter came along. Fred was best man.

They were married in the chapel at Balliol. Annabel wore flowers in her hair, but no veil. The service, the music and the prayers were all in keeping with the medieval building, which made Handel's Wedding March seem almost modern. Nothing could make Annabel seem anything other than what she was: a stunningly beautiful girl on the verge of a great adventure. The huge blue eyes looked up at her husband with such rapture that it seemed very likely that she would devour him on the spot when the vicar pronounced them man and wife:

"You may kiss the bride."

"Steady, Tiger," whispered Rick.

-§-

The reception was at Walmer House, in the large but neglected conservatory. It was an old-fashioned Victorian affair that leaked so much that when it rained

Road trip Isfahan 1969

the plants got watered. It wasn't made to sit in, but to grow rare and exotic plants.

"You're a rare and exotic plant, Annabel," he told her.

"Then you'll have to pay me special attention, Rick."

The plants had been moved into the garden for the day and a long refectory table placed down the middle. The vine stayed, giving shade and an almost Mediterranean air to the proceedings.

The father of the bride spoke about losing a daughter but gaining a son-in-law. Rick was so drunk he slipped under the table. The best man unsteadily gripped a pillar and started a speech that made out that Annabel was a little tart. Groans, clucking noises and sniggers went round. Annabel stood up and with unswerving aim laid him out cold with a bottle of champagne. Blood tricked onto the antique tiles from an open head wound.

"Call an ambulance!" shouted Rick's father.

"Get a doctor!" called an uncle.

Annabel emptied a jug of cold water over Rick and tweaked his nose.

"Wake up! Time to go to work!"

Shock and pain had the desired effect and Annabel watched as her husband crawled over to the victim and staunched the bleeding with a napkin. Then he opened Fred's eyes with two fingers and rolled his head from side to side. Apparently satisfied with what he saw he raised Fred's legs and carefully placed them on a chair.

"Don't let him sit up just yet."

But Fred was having none of it. Getting onto all fours, he gripped a chair with determination, pulled

Road trip Isfahan 1969

himself to his feet and burst into song just as the ambulance arrived.

"In Old England jolly good times," he bellowed.

"Take him away," shouted the ladies.

"He's fine now, the doctor has sorted him," said the men.

The Ambulance crew looked confused.

"Shall we call the police?" they asked nobody in particular.

Rick seemed quite sober now.

"No need for that. The ladies just panicked when they saw the blood, but the wound is only superficial."

The bemused guests settled down to eat the feast, which finished with crème brûlée.

Charlotte sidled up to Rick.

"Do you remember another crème brûlée?" she asked. "I seem to recall that you were rather partial to the stuff."

"Indeed I am, Charlotte, and I have some startling memories of that evening, bitter sweet you might say."

"Why didn't you contact me? I waited and waited."

"Because I was still in love with Annabel, simple as that. I thought you and Peter had something going when Maddie had her fling with your brother?"

"Yes but that didn't work out either."

"Oh Charlotte, I'm sorry to hear that. But you have always got your brother to fall back on. It seems to me he remains your best friend."

"He and I have loved each other since we were just kids."

"Brother Sun, Sister Moon?"

Road trip Isfahan 1969

"Yes! Just like in ancient Egypt. Don't all sisters imagine they are going to marry their brothers, until they turn twelve?"

Annabel came up behind Charlotte and put her arms around her. She whispered:

"Leave my man alone Charlotte or I will brain you. There is still plenty of champagne left!"

Rick moved swiftly behind Annabel and grabbed her around the waist.

"Come on my one and only true love, I want to dance."

They pushed back the tables and danced till dawn. The last guests drifted away, disappointed not to be able to watch the bride and groom leave for their honeymoon. Elizabeth explained that the happy couple had gone upstairs to bed. They were in Annabel's room fast asleep in each other's arms, although only half undressed.

The honeymoon started next day. Annabel drove them down to Brighton and they checked into an hotel overlooking the Palace Pier. Rick slept most of the way.

-§-

With their parents help, Annabel and Rick bought a two-bedroom terraced house just off Lavender Hill, almost exactly halfway between Battersea Park and Clapham Common. The Mini was parked in the street. They had only just moved in. It was still the summer holidays and Rick was on leave.

"I'm not going to take the tube to work, Rick. It means changing twice. It's OK for you. You can walk to

Road trip Isfahan 1969

Clapham Common and take the Northern line straight there."

"Drive then; staff can park in the school grounds, can't they?"

After Kensington Church Street, it seemed like they had unlimited space. They went upstairs and into the small bedroom. Annabel opened the sash window that looked out over their backyard and onto the neighbours. Yellow paper was peeling off the wall.

"I am going to start decorating in here. Wallpaper with balloons and clowns and a blue ceiling with stars."

"Yes, the North Star surrounded by Cassiopeia and Orion."

"And don't forget the Great Bear."

Annabel flung her arms around his neck and held on tight.

"I'm so excited."

They changed and went for a run on the Common and squashed into the shower together.

"I'll call up Fred and ask him to meet us in the Windmill."

Rick was on the phone while Annabel was putting on her make-up, wearing a towel round her head and nothing else.

"He says: 'Can he bring Diana?'" Rick shouted up the stairs.

"Of course he can. Tell them to come fully armed, there be monsters south of the river."

Rick put the phone down.

"We must have an extension in the bedroom. I can't go running up and down the stairs when I'm on-call."

Chapter Twenty
Annabel's Illness

Rick came home after a long day at the hospital. Annabel was lying on the sofa; she looked washed out. She wasn't even watching TV. He walked over and bent to kiss her.

"You look awful, Sugar. Did you get to see Dr Jacobs?"

"No he couldn't fit me in but I saw a locum GP. She was really nice; she couldn't find anything wrong but she did run some tests. And Rick don't call me Sugar, you only call me that when you're worried."

Rick laughed, but he was worried: he had felt her abdomen when she complained of terrible pains in the night; he had found an enlarged spleen and she had been having nose bleeds. He was sick with worry and he could tell that despite putting on a brave face she was frightened, that was why he was home early. He was glad the GP has sent off the bloods, now he was just waiting for the phone to ring.

When the call came, it was a female voice that asked to speak to Mrs Griffin. He carried the phone over to her, and watched her anxiously as she took the call.

"Yes, yes," she was saying. "I'll go along tomorrow, at midday, Clinic C2, Dr. Marsden," she put the phone the down.

He sat beside her, his arm around her.

"They've found something haven't they," she said.

Her big blue eyes sought his face. She looked scared. He didn't answer, tears welled up, he couldn't speak.

Road trip Isfahan 1969

They clung together. She seemed to be comforting him rather than the other way around. At last she said:
"Come on, this is getting us nowhere. Cup o' tea?"
"Don't you want something stronger?"
"Alcohol is not going to get us through this, Rick."

-§-

The Consultant saw them at the end of clinic, he looked tired, holding out his hand he introduced himself to Annabel:
"David Marsden. I'm your consultant."
He was wearing a badge. It said his name and underneath: Consultant Haematologist, not too threatening, and his grey hair was somehow reassuring, Rick thought. Annabel smiled brightly, he could tell that she was hoping the diagnosis would be nothing too bad, they both were. Dr Marsden motioned them to chairs which were placed at an angle to his desk. When he sat down their knees were almost touching. He learnt forwards and looked at Annabel intently:
"What do you know?"
Annabel swallowed and smiled.
"My mouth is a bit dry...."
The doctor signalled to a nurse who had been standing quietly in a corner, now she stepped forwards, as if on cue, with a plastic cup of water. The nurse sat down beside Annabel and held her hand. Annabel withdrew it and looked straight at the doctor.
"I've got something wrong with my blood, haven't I? Haematology is about blood disorders, isn't it?"

Road trip Isfahan 1969

"The tests show you've got leukaemia. Too many immature white cells in the blood," he paused and smiled.

Annabel was pale already, now she turned even paler. She seemed to be thinking. The doctor waited.

"Is that cancer? I'm a teacher, not a doctor."

"Yes, it is a type of cancer of the blood."

"But it is treatable, isn't it? I mean people with leukaemia nearly all survive now, don't they?"

She turned to Rick who took her hand but looked down, biting his lip.

"Of course, of course, there is very good treatment."

Dr Marsden nodded as if to emphasise his words.

Rick blew his nose:

"What sort of leukaemia is it?" he asked.

"It is T-cell leukaemia, at least that's what we think at present, samples have been sent away for biological markers and so on. If you can stay in, we will start treatment tomorrow."

"Yes, I can stay." Annabel was looking down at her hands.

"Do you have things you have to do at home?"

"No. Rick can tell them at work."

"Any children?"

"No," said Rick.

Annabel started to cry silently, tears poured down her cheeks.

"No children," she whispered and shook her head.

The nurse put her arms around Annabel.

"Plenty of time for that later… eh? Get through the treatment and then you can think about having a family."

Road trip Isfahan 1969

"Nurse Millicent will take you to the ward. If you have any questions, ask the ward staff to contact me. I am usually around and if I'm not my registrar, Sarah Jones, is always ready to step into the breach. I trust her completely," said Dr Marsden.

"Thank you, doctor," said Annabel, she didn't look up.

He leant forwards and looked into her face.

"Call me David. We're all on first name terms in this team. Remember that I'm here to look after you, and so is Sarah and so is Millie; you're going to get through this."

Millie took Annabel's arm as if to help her to her feet and led her out of the clinic. Rick followed, too numb to be able to think clearly or feel anything.

-§-

As a courtesy to a doctor's wife Annabel was put in a side ward by herself. The first night she was on an intravenous infusion and given drugs to protect the kidneys.

Rick went home to the house on Lavender Hill. It was hard to concentrate. There was so much to do but he could not decide where to start. He went upstairs to get her toothbrush and nightie, but sat on the bed and cried. He went downstairs and put the kettle on the gas, realised he had left the things upstairs. By the bed he saw the telephone and remembered he must phone the school, he was listening to the ring tone when the kettle started to whistle so he put the receiver down and ran back to the kitchen. He made himself a cup of tea and sat

Road trip Isfahan 1969

staring at the wall. Oh, God, T-cell leukaemia, not a good prognosis. It was quite likely that she would never come home. Induction therapy killed nearly as many patients as it saved. Tears poured down his face. The tea was stone cold; he must get a grip. He tried phoning the school again but they had all gone home. He found a bag and stuffed her things into it. He picked up her teddy and put it down again. He went back to the phone and tried his brother.

"Hello, hello? Who is it?"

Rick put the receiver back in its cradle unable to speak, unable to say the dreadful words that would make this nightmare real. He got into the car. Outside the hospital he sat behind the wheel and took deep breaths. Steady the buffs, it was easier for him because at least he knew his way around. He understood the jargon, and being here felt like being at work, he could almost detach himself from the personal drama that was unfolding, at home there was no such support. He smiled, stepped out of the car and made for the ward.

"Here's my husband. This is Sarah," said Annabel.

"Hi Sarah," said Rick.

He had noticed her in the canteen, tall, dark haired, with a Roman nose and a Welsh lilt to her voice, but he hardly knew her.

"I'm glad you're here I was just talking to Annabel about fertility and side effects of chemotherapy."

Rick nodded, never too soon to grasp the nettle. But it did seem a bit brutal having this conversation on day one. Dr Jones seemed to read his mind.

"I know this is not the time you would choose to talk about babies, I realise that you are both in shock, but I'm

Road trip Isfahan 1969

afraid there is no time to lose. We must start treatment in the next few days and as I was saying to Annabel when you came in, the medicines will reduce fertility so harvesting some eggs now is a wise precaution."

She stopped to let her words sink in. Rick nodded, Annabel stared at her.

"Oh no," she said. "Do I have to have those drugs?"

Rick sat on the bed and put his arms around her:

"Yes you do, Sugar. You must. You must. It is the best chance of a complete cure."

Their tears mingled as he pressed his cheek to hers. Dr Jones remained calm and professional. She reached out and held Annabel's hand and waited. At last, after what seemed like an age she said.

"You have a wonderful husband, Annabel and I can see he is going to support you through this."

She paused again and waited for Annabel to respond.

"Yes," she whispered. "Yes. Go on I am listening now, and I do want to know what is best, I really do."

"Tomorrow, I have arranged for Mr Rix our surgeon, to take a snip out of one of your ovaries, so that we can freeze the eggs. Then if you want to have babies when you're better, they will be there, if you need them. That is if you consent to the procedure. It is a bit like having your appendix out."

She went on to explain the operation in more detail and mentioned bleeding as a complication.

"Could she have her appendix out at the same time?" asked Rick.

"That is an idea; my experience is that Mr Rix is not keen on doing operations unless they are really necessary, but I will ask him."

Road trip Isfahan 1969

"You mentioned bleeding. Are her platelets ok?" asked Rick.

Dr Jones laughed.

"I am the doctor and you are the husband. We worry about the numbers; your job is to worry about Annabel."

"Sorry," said Rick. "It's a sort of reflex."

"Now Annabel, while you are asleep we will also take some bone marrow through a large needle from the top of your pelvis, and put another needle into your back to take some spinal fluid and inject Methotrexate to protect your brain from the leukaemia."

Dr Jones passed the consent form to Annabel who signed it, without asking any more questions.

"Overnight, Annabel, you are going to continue with the intravenous fluids and drugs to protect your kidneys. Then in the morning Mr Rix will do his bit, and when we are happy that all is well, we will start you on chemotherapy. I know it is all too much to take in just now, but I'll be back tomorrow and please write down any questions you may have for me."

When the registrar had gone, Rick settled into a chair by the bed. He closed his eyes.

"Tired, my lovely?" asked Annabel.

Rick shook himself and smiled at her.

"Why are you mocking Sarah? I thought she was really kind," said Rick.

"She is and I love her accent, she speaks so clearly," Annabel replied.

"I think you two are going to get on just great."

"Do you know her from work?"

"No. ENT is a world away from Haematology and Oncology, our paths rarely cross."

Road trip Isfahan 1969

"What are you going to do now?"

"I'll go to the canteen for supper and then sleep in this chair tonight."

"No, Rick, go home. I'll be fine."

"I can't face the house without you. I'm happier here tonight."

The nurse came in with food for Annabel and Rick went down to the canteen.

-§-

"I'll pop home for a bath."

It was 6am and the night staff were doing a drug round before going off duty.

"Yes, my lovely you certainly need one. You look and smell like something the cat found in the dung heap."

"I won't kiss you then," said Rick but got out of the sweaty chair and kissed her anyway.

He was just leaving when Mr Rix rushed in.

"Oh my word! They said you're beautiful, but I see they were wrong! You are exquisitely beautiful. I'm Mr Rix your surgeon. I've only come to introduce myself and to say I'll put in a long line while you're asleep. Technically it's called a Hickman."

He took a felt pen and drew a line under Annabel's collar bone where the cannula was going to go. If you have any questions just fire away!"

He beamed at his patient and handed her the pen to sign another consent form. Annabel just smiled and then managed a very quiet:

"None, thank you."

Road trip Isfahan 1969

He smiled back and left.

"Oh my God, Rick! Is he always like that?"

"Only with all his patients. He doesn't mean anything by it; he says the same thing to young and old alike. He thinks it cheers them up."

"I think he's right. It made me want to laugh but I thought that might offend him."

"Impossible to offend a surgeon; they have hides like a rhino. I better get going."

-§-

"Hi, Tom."

Far away at the other end of the line in Oxford.

"Hi, Rick, what's up?" Tom sounded surprised.

Rick never normally rang him; they were not the best of friends.

"Hi, I was going to ring your mum, but then thought I'd better ring you first."

"Why? Is it about Annabel?"

"Yes. She's not well."

"Not well? What do you mean?"

"It's leukaemia."

There, the word was out now, it could not be taken back. The word hovered in the air, in the wires, between them, a huge dense malignant force. There was silence.

"Tom?"

"Yes, I'm here. Will she be alright?"

"Well the doctors say it's a T-cell leukaemia, which does not have the best prognosis."

Road trip Isfahan 1969

"For God's sake Rick, speak English, can't you? I know you're a doctor but what are you saying in plain language?"

He sounded angry and Rick felt even more anxious about telling the truth.

"It's bad, Tom. She might die, the chances are about 50/50."

Tears welled up and he couldn't speak.

"Then she might live, look on the bright side Rick. She's got to live. She's my little sister and nothing ever gets the better of her, of course she's going to live, you fool. Don't ever, ever, even for a minute think otherwise."

"Thank you Tom, please can you tell your mum?"

The line went dead. Next he phoned Medical Staffing, told them he needed to take leave and that he would come in that afternoon to tell them the details. They sounded surprised but he cut them off. Not able to face anymore telephone calls, he ran a bath and shaved while the water splashed into the tub.

-§-

When he got back to the ward he found Nurse Millicent changing Annabel's drip.

"Hi Nurse, I didn't think you worked here, I thought you were in Out Patients."

"I go where my patients are, Rick. We are all on first name terms here, call me Millie."

"So you'll be around when Annabel has her chemo?"

Road trip Isfahan 1969

"Yes, I help check the chemo and set it up. The ward staff are very good but they appreciate my help when, like now, they are so busy."

It was difficult to know if Annabel was listening. Her eyes were shut and her breathing was quite shallow.

"She's only just back from theatres. The anaesthetic has not completely worn off yet," said Millie.

On the second day, the chemotherapy started. True to her word Millie was there connecting the bright red fluid to the Hickman line. She took off her gloves and sat on the bed, watching the fluid run through, checking the rate.

"The next two weeks are tough, but then you will be through the worst. You will have daily infusions as well as medicines by mouth."

Annabel looked frightened. "Stop, Millie. Rick understands this stuff, but I'm a teacher."

"Can we have a look at the protocol?" asked Rick.

"Yes of course, I was going to give you your diary tomorrow but I'll get it now."

She came back with a ring binder and opened it. Rick stood beside the bed, looking over Annabel's shoulder. They stared at the flow charts, while Millie did her best to explain things.

Annabel fell back on the pillows.

"You were quite right, Millie. It is all too much for me to take in now but I hope I will feel stronger soon."

Millie and Rick exchanged glances. Rick knew that Annabel was only likely to feel worse over the days to come.

-§-

Road trip Isfahan 1969

As predicted the chemotherapy took its toll: Annabel vomited after each infusion and stopped eating altogether. Mouth ulcers and thrush added to her misery.

"You're so brave, Sugar." Rick rocked her in his arms.

She was given the strongest medicines to combat the side effects, but they in turn had side effects: she slept most of the time. Her bone marrow stopped putting out malignant cells, but it also stopped making normal cells. She had to have transfusions of blood and platelets.

"Platelets?" asked Annabel. "What are platelets, please?"

Sarah was helping Millie set up the infusion, while writing up more drugs.

"The small ones that stop you bleeding."

Annabel shook her head, and shut her eyes, tears rolled down her cheeks.

"I'm sorry," she said.

"Don't be sorry, darling," whispered Rick. "It's not your fault. You've done nothing wrong."

Dr Jones smiled and patted him on the shoulder.

"She's doing great. A few more days and we will be though the induction phase."

"What then?" asked Rick.

"We will do another bone marrow examination and if that shows remission, we can start maintenance treatment."

-§-

Road trip Isfahan 1969

"The bone marrow shows just a few blasts now, less than 10% is regarded as satisfactory," said Dr Marsden.

Annabel and Rick were sitting side by side in his clinic, her dressing gown covered her nightie. She was still an inpatient.

"We'll give you an injection of Vincristine and start five days of Pred. Then you can go home this afternoon," he smiled brightly. "I bet you are longing to get home."

Annabel smiled back.

"When will the other medicines on the schedule start?" asked Rick.

"When we have count recovery, when the neutrophils reach one, in other words. Until then there is a real risk of infection, septicaemia. If your temperature rises above 38°C or you feel unwell, cold and shivery, then you must come straight back here. Any delay could be very serious."

Although Rick had asked the question Dr Marsden was looking intently at Annabel all the time he was talking. She closed her eyes and her lips quivered.

"Neutrophils? Septicaemia? What if I do get septicaemia? What does very serious mean? I just don't understand."

She blinked back tears then hid her face in her hands. Millie put her arms around her shoulders, Dr Marsden held her hand. Rick patted her knee.

"I'm sorry. I did not mean to frighten you. You're doing really well, I am so pleased with your progress," said the Consultant.

"You've been so brave, love," said Millie.

"Come on Sugar, you'll feel better once you're home," said Rick.

Road trip Isfahan 1969

Annabel raised her head.
"Don't you Sugar me Rick!"
"That's the spirit, you tell him!" said Dr Marsden.
Rick smiled, underneath it all the real Annabel was still there.
"Who will be at home?" asked Millie.
"I will. I have taken what Medical Staffing call compassionate leave and I am not going to look for another job until Annabel is out of the woods."

-§-

Rick offered to do Annabel's daily blood tests, but Millie was quite shocked:
"No you will not Rick! Your job is to look after your wife. Do some cooking and cleaning, go shopping; do not try to doctor her! We have a community nurse who will come in to see to that side of things."

Another week and Annabel's count had recovered enough to start the medicines by mouth. They began to understand the jargon and even established a routine.

"I've got used to having you at home," said Annabel. "It almost seems like we are living a normal life."

It was morning and she was sitting on the bed after her shower. Rick was drying her hair, as he brushed, it came out in handfuls. They had been told to expect this but it still came as an awful blow. Annabel was surprisingly cheerful.

"I'll get a wig, no, two wigs!"

They went to the wig maker and ordered one which was a mass of blonde curls and another of straight black hair that was so long it hung all down her back.

Road trip Isfahan 1969

The morning the wigs arrived, she put them on and danced about the bedroom.

"Which do you like best?" she asked him "Dolly Parton or Joan Baez?"

"You. I love you. I don't care what you look like."

In truth, he wanted her long straight blonde hair back, and this whole nightmare to be over. She seemed so much stronger than him. Now she was waltzing around the room singing about a lonesome valley, apparently unaware of the irony. Suddenly she stopped and came and sat beside him.

"Hold me," she said. "Never let me go."

-§-

The daily blood tests became weekly and visits to the hospital became monthly for the lumbar puncture, and the intravenous vincristine. There were weeks when her count was too low and the medicines were stopped and an incident during one such week when they rushed back to the hospital because she had a high temperature and could not stop shivering. That meant days in hospital while the infection was treated with triple intravenous antibiotics, which in turn meant complications, like thrush.

"You're doing so well. You're my star patient!" said Dr Marsden.

He said that every time he saw them.

"Thank you," said Annabel. "How much longer will the treatment go on? According to the protocol, I'll be finished soon."

Road trip Isfahan 1969

"Another month and we'll do the final bone marrow. Then it's just a question of follow up visits."

-§-

The follow up visits were becoming a bore. There was the result of the blood test, and then Dr Marsden would ask her to jump up on the couch. Annabel lay down and pulled up her t-shirt so that the doctor could feel for a spleen. He talked as he examined her.

"All's well. Platelets a bit low but that's nothing to worry about."

"When can we start trying for a family?" she asked.

"Well, your immune system will take about two years to fully recover so I would wait a bit," was his evasive reply.

Annabel smiled. Rick helped her down off the couch. She didn't meet his eye; he could tell she was disappointed. On the way out, they bumped into Dr Jones.

"Annabel, well both of us, actually, want to start a family. What do you think?" said Rick.

"Yes! Why not?" said the registrar.

Annabel beamed at her.

-§-

"I'm home!" called Rick

"How did the interview go?"

"Got the job. I'm starting 1st June."

"Peering up noses and into lug holes! What fun!" said Annabel.

Road trip Isfahan 1969

"Better than peering into other orifices, I can tell you. I never liked General Surgery."

"And you'll be dealing with children a lot of the time."

She put her arms around his neck and pulled him down for a kiss.

"I've been monitoring my temperature and I think tonight is the night! So, no drink for you!"

"No celebrating the new job?"

"Yes, of course we will. I've got a chicken in the oven, and I'll open a bottle orange juice."

"The sooner you have a bun in the oven and I can have a drink, the better."

He smiled at her.

"You don't find me boring, do you?"

"Never!"

He carried her upstairs and threw her on the bed.

-§-

"How did Parents evening go?" Rick smiled up at Annabel, she looked exhausted, but it had been a very long day. It was unusual for him to be home first. He was guiltily sipping a glass of wine. She frowned.

"Oh all the usual complaints. Johnny's mum was cross because he's been kept down a year. Suzy's dad was furious because his daughter is not in the hockey team. And I'm not even the games mistress! Really parents are impossible."

She threw herself down on the sofa beside him.

"Can I get you something, a very weak gin perhaps?"

Road trip Isfahan 1969

It was not like Annabel to complain like this. She must be feeling very low. He knew he'd said the wrong thing as soon as it was out of his mouth but it was only because he wanted to cheer her up. His remark had the opposite effect. She flared up.

"You know I'm not drinking."

He put his arms around her.

"I'm sorry," he said "What's the matter? What's getting to you?"

"Oh Rick, I just want a baby, I want a baby so much."

"It'll happen, lovely. I'm sure it will."

Tears were pouring down.

"But I feel so ill."

-§-

Dr Marsden looked serious as he palpated Annabel's abdomen.

"There are a few immature cells in the blood count," he remarked.

He went back to his desk and Rick helped Annabel down off the couch. She had looked pale these last few days.

"You'll have to come in for some tests."

He waited, watching her carefully. Annabel stared at him and said nothing. Rick bit his tongue. The silence seemed to go on for ever.

"I know," said Annabel at last. "I've known for a while now."

Road trip Isfahan 1969

The flood gates opened. She clung to Rick and he to her. Dr Marsden produced a box of Kleenex from a drawer, and Millie hurried off to make cups of tea.

-§-

"How's my lovely today?" asked Dr Jones.

"Very well thank you!" said Annabel brightly.

Dr Jones seemed to be the one in charge now. Dr Marsden had withdrawn.

"He hates it when patients relapse, and as he gets older he finds it harder," she explained.

"Odd that, you'd think it would be easier, the more experienced you are," said Rick.

"Well, of course he knows everything that is happening but he tells me that I am the one who is the real expert in these matters."

Rick got the impression that perhaps Dr Jones was hiding something, but he did not want to challenge her in front of Annabel.

Annabel was putting on a brave face, Rick could tell.

"Second time around it's easier, because I know what to expect and I understand the jargon now," she said.

"But the medicines are all different this time," objected Rick.

He was still working, but the on-call was not too onerous and his Consultant let him leave clinic early on days that Annabel had chemo. The drugs she was taking were much stronger this time and he was amazed how Annabel coped with the side effects which were more severe than before. He caught up with Dr Jones in the canteen.

"Hi, my lovely!" called out the irrepressible oncology registrar in her Welsh accent.

"I bet you say that to all the boys," responded Rick.

"Well I do, actually, but you're still my favourite."

"Don't tease Sarah, I want to ask you a serious question."

"Fire away!"

"I'm worried that Annabel hasn't gone into remission. When will we know?"

"The bone marrow is booked for tomorrow, that will tell us. Her platelets are low so I've ordered a unit to cover the procedure."

"Is it usual for the platelets to be so low at this point.?"

Sarah made a see-saw gesture with her hands.

"Yes it's to be expected, but there are other things that make me worry, I will not pretend that all is going quite as well as I hoped. But at the moment it's just a feeling in my water!"

She smiled encouragingly.

-§-

"How are you feeling, Sugar?"

Rick was standing by the bed; a unit of platelets were running in through the Hickman line. Annabel was dreadfully pale, but she managed a smile.

"Sore," she closed her eyes.

"Where? has the local anaesthetic worn off?"

"No, just all over."

Road trip Isfahan 1969

"Shall I read to you?"

Rick opened the book and started but Annabel raised her hand and signalled to him to stop.

"I just want to sleep," she whispered.

He slid down in the chair and shut his eyes, they could both do with some sleep. He was woken by Dr Jones.

"Hi Sarah, what's up?"

Dr Jones was locking off the Hickman with a heparin flush.

"Dr Marsden will be along in a minute. He has got something rather important to discuss with you both."

Annabel sat up and looked about her. Dr Jones plumped up her pillows and tried to make her comfortable. Millie came in, lugging two chairs.

"Hey! That's my job," she said, and took over straightening the sheets. It became clear that this whole dance had been carefully choreographed. Dr Marsden came in and sat on the bed, while the others sat a little way back, waiting to hear what he had to say.

"I've been looking at your bone marrow. It's stuffed with blasts, that's why you are so tired and your blood counts are so low."

Rick let out involuntary groan and reached for Annabel's hand. She gripped him with surprising force and dug her nails into his palm, he didn't notice. Despite the jargon this did not sound good. Dr Marsden waited, it was as if the whole room was holding its breath, wondering what Annabel would say.

"Blasts?" her voice was low but controlled. "Blasts are malignant cells, aren't they? You're telling me the cancer has come back?"

Dr Marsden nodded and patted her leg through the bed clothes.

"What are the options?" asked Rick.

The Consultant straightened up and still looking at Annabel said:

"There is a lot we can do, but complete remission is not something that we can hope for now."

He looked at Dr Jones. Sarah got up and came forwards to sit opposite him on the bed.

"I'm going to arrange a blood transfusion, that will make you feel a lot better, and then I'm going to start a diamorphine infusion that will take away the pain."

"Can I go home?"

"Yes, just as soon as I have arranged the pump for the diamorphine and alerted the community nurses to the plan."

"Tomorrow then?"

"Yes, Annabel, tomorrow."

"Rick," she said. "Rick, you'll look after me, won't you?"

"I'll sleep here tonight, Sugar, and then we will get you home."

Then, turning to the nurse, he said: "Millie, can you stay here while I sort out Medical Staffing? They'll have to arrange a locum."

-§-

"Can I mend Teddy for you?" asked Rick.

Annabel clutched her bear to her; he had one eye missing. Rick was holding up a black bead. It wasn't

Road trip Isfahan 1969

Teddy's original eye but it would do; he would look less forlorn.

"No, you can't mend him. Nobody can."

He lay down beside her and shut his eyes. They tried to doze. He was roused by the alarm on the syringe driver; time to change the diamorphine.

They were both exhausted; over the weeks they had not had one uninterrupted night, and when they did sleep they tossed and turned; he had dragged a single mattress into their bedroom and lay down on that at night.

"Do you want anything? Tea and toast? Lemon squash?"

"No, I'm fine thank you."

He helped her rinse her mouth and went to get the medicine and more ice cubes. While in the kitchen he boiled the kettle and looked in the fridge for something to tempt her appetite. She had lost so much weight that he could see her skull beneath her skin. When he helped her wash, her bones were painfully prominent; it was only by constant attention to pressure areas and the use of creams and sheepskins that they avoided bedsores.

"I'm going to increase the base rate, and you need to boost more often. Don't be brave, Sugar, don't suffer in silence."

"I'm not suffering. I really am fine, just a bit tired."

She shut her eyes; he could tell she was only pretending to sleep in order to shut him up. He sat in a chair and sipped his tea, watching her. At last her breathing became regular and she slept. He went downstairs to fix himself scrambled eggs.

-§-

Road trip Isfahan 1969

Rick paced back and forth between the bedroom windows. Annabel was sitting in the armchair in her pyjamas. The Tintin motif made her look vulnerable, childlike. They were waiting for her mother and Tom. Rick kept looking down into the street.

"Are you cold, Sugar? Do you want your dressing gown?"

"I'm fine Rick, in fact it's stuffy in here."

The heating was turned right up even though it was early autumn. He opened a window as the Volvo drew up outside. He was at the front door open before they could ring the bell.

"Hi Tom, Elizabeth. Come in, come in."

Annabel was standing at the top of the stairs holding onto the banisters.

"Don't jump!" called Rick.

Tom held out his arms, but Rick quickly reached her side and put his arms around her to help her down.

"Hello, darling, I'm glad to see you are up and about. I thought you would be confined to bed," said Elizabeth.

"No Mum, I'm quite capable of coming downstairs."

Rick helped Annabel onto the sofa and her mother sat beside her, while Rick and Tom went into the kitchen to make tea and cut up the cake, cooked that morning in an uncharacteristic burst of domesticity by Elizabeth.

"Annabel seems to be so well. I didn't expect to see her up and about," said Tom.

"She's making a special effort. Before you came she was on a morphine infusion to control the pain. She stopped it only because you're here."

Road trip Isfahan 1969

"Oh my God, I can't believe it. She was never ill when she lived at home," said Tom.

They didn't stay long. Annabel was too weak to climb the stairs; Rick carried her back to bed and reconnected the diamorphine, giving the syringe two boosts. She looked grey with pain and exhaustion. The effort of pretending to her mother and Tom that she was coping had taken its toll.

-§-

"Hi Millie, how are you this morning?"

"I've brought Sarah with me to review the medication, Rick."

Dr Jones appeared swinging her bag.

"Morning Rick, how's my patient?"

"Annabel's fine. She sleeps a bit and she's not in pain. I've increased the rate on the pump, just as you said."

"How are you?"

"I'm OK, bit sleep deprived, but OK, thank you."

Dr Jones nodded. They went upstairs. Annabel had turned her face to the wall, and was apparently asleep.

"Morning sleepy head."

Dr Jones very gently shook her by the shoulder. Annabel turned over with difficulty.

"How do you get to the bathroom, lovely?"

"Rick carries me, and puts me in the bath, or on the loo or whatever."

"Your doing so well, I'm so proud of you both, aren't we Millie?"

"Yes, we are!" said Millie.

Road trip Isfahan 1969

Annabel grimaced.

"I'm going to talk to Rick downstairs, just to make sure you have all you need."

"I'll say goodbye then Sarah. I don't suppose I'll be seeing you again. Please look after Rick."

-§-

Millie and the community nurses laid her out in her wedding dress, and put a bunch of white flowers in her hands. Rick looked down on her in her coffin; in death she had regained the transparent beauty that in life people had so admired. The funeral directors screwed down the lid and took her away. When the nurses had gone and the house was empty, Rick went upstairs, sat on the unmade bed and cried. He was numb with pain and exhaustion.

-§-

The funeral service was in the chapel at Balliol, where they had been married. Rick stood between Tom and her father, mother next to Tom, his parents and his sister in the pew opposite. At the back of the chapel a few student friends had crept in, including Charlotte and Charles. It was a conventional Church of England service. Tom read out a few words about his sister, Rick had declined the invitation to speak. The priest recited a eulogy:

"She was clever and beautiful and above all kind. She had a strong moral compass........."

"What next!" whispered Rick to Tom. "I hate this kind of stuff. He didn't know her at all!"

Road trip Isfahan 1969

"Shush," Tom murmured.

They buried her in the cemetery on the hill overlooking Oxford. The spires were obscured by rain. Rick was standing beside her father.

"In her mind Oxford was always home, she never became a Londoner. I'm glad she is buried here overlooking her city," said Rick.

Chapter Twenty-One
Rick Leaves London
1985

The next six months were hard. Rick was given compassionate leave. He should have been busy sorting things out. But concentrating was difficult and he got almost nothing done. He spent the evenings wandering around the house, whispering her name over and over again, and crying tears that never seemed to dry up. Then he would fall into an exhausted sleep. Medical friends advised him to take something but the little blue pills made him feel numb, tired and confused so he stopped them. Sarah and Millie wanted to visit but he refused to see them. He lied, telling them he was just fine and didn't need their help. He lay in bed in the mornings and tried to plan the day ahead, but he finished up thinking about Annabel and crying. When he did get up the sight of his sore red eyes in the mirror put him off shaving so he grew a stubbly beard. It made him look unkempt and neglected and he was losing weight but he was past caring. Tom offered to drive up to town and help him sort out Annabel's things but Rick told him to stay away. When the time came to get back to work he realised that he would not be able to face the hospital and his colleagues and resigned.

Rick went round to an estate agent on Lavender Hill and asked him to let the house, furnished. Then he went home and loaded Annabel's clothes, her shoes and her teddy into two huge suitcases. His own clothes he forced into a large rucksack. He loaded up Annabel's Mini and drove up to Oxford. As he approached Walmer House,

Road trip Isfahan 1969

panic seized him and he had to stop the car, while sobs shook him and he howled in pain.

A short girl with dark hair tied back in a ponytail, tapped on the glass of the Mini and made a gesture meaning wind down the window. Rick stared at her and then complied. She didn't seem frightened, but looked at him as if she understood.

"Can I help?" she asked. "You look like you could do with someone to talk to."

"I'm looking for Walmer House. It's in Rawlinson Road."

She nodded. "I know. That family has had an awful tragedy. They lost their daughter. You're Annabel's husband returning her things. You're hurting now but you're strong. You'll be alright."

She turned and swinging her bag, walked away. Rick stared after her but she just faded from sight. He smiled through his tears, and shook his head.

Tom answered the door.

"My God Rick, you do look pale."

"Yeah, I think I have just seen a ghost." He paused, then added: "where's Elizabeth?"

"She taken to her bed. She doesn't get up much now."

They took the two suitcases upstairs and hung the dresses in Annabel's wardrobe. Rick put her teddy on her pillow. The room was exactly as she had left it.

"You haven't even changed the sheets," said Rick.

"Mum says nothing, absolutely nothing, is to be touched."

Road trip Isfahan 1969

Rick took the Mini to a local garage and sold it back to the man Annabel had bought it from. Then he bought himself a powerful motorbike, a Honda 750 Four.

-§-

Months later, Rick got back to work and the following summer found him in Brighton, a busy ENT registrar. In the canteen, he met Dr Sarah Jones. It was the first time he had seen her since Annabel died, and he felt awkward, unsure how she would react to seeing him again. Her back was turned to him; she was standing by the food counter, contemplating the unappetising dishes on offer.

"Hi, Sarah!"

She turned and stared at him as if not sure who had called her name. Then she smiled.

"I didn't expect to see you!"

"I didn't know you were working here either."

"I've been here a month now."

"What are you doing exactly?"

"Working in Haematology as ever, but now I am a Consultant."

"Well, congratulations Sarah, I am impressed."

They went over to a table and sat opposite each other.

"What are you eating?" asked Rick slicing up his bangers and pushing the gravy and mashed potato around the plate.

"Sweetbreads," answered Sarah.

"Oh goodness, how can you? Is that brain, testes or pancreas?"

Road trip Isfahan 1969

Sarah laughed. "Tell me where you've been."

"After Annabel died I more or less had a nervous breakdown. I didn't want to go home and I didn't want to be around Annabel's friends. I felt guilty, I don't know why."

"Why didn't you go home?" she asked.

"Well, my parents never understood Annabel. She was too Bohemian for them I guess. My mum actually said Annabel's short dresses made her look like a tart."

"What did your dad think?"

"Oh, he liked her because she was so beautiful, but he was intimidated at the same time. We hardly ever went to see them."

"And you didn't like her brother Tom much, did you?"

"The feeling was mutual. I think Tom and Elizabeth somehow blamed me for Annabel's death."

"Oh?" Sarah raised her eyebrows.

"In a way they reinforced the thoughts that kept me awake me night after night. As a doctor and the closest person to her, I should have realised that she was ill far sooner and then she would have started treatment earlier and survived."

Rick's voice quavered and he blinked back tears.

"Let's get out of here," said Sarah.

They walked across the car park and got into her red MGB. She set off in the direction of Devil's Dyke. Rick looked out of the window, ashamed of showing his feelings so easily. Sarah drove confidently, double de-clutching on the steep bends up to the Dyke.

"Haven't you got anything to do this afternoon?" Rick asked.

"No that's the great thing about being the new consultant, my timetable is not overcrowded, yet."

"Ditto," he said. "I am supposed to be in the office this afternoon, but I haven't any reports to write today."

"Where did you go? You just disappeared, Millie and I asked around but no one seemed to know."

They wandered along the edge of the Dyke: the Sussex Weald and the village of Fulking was spread out like a map below them. Hang gliders were landing and taking off.

"I'd love to do that," said Sarah, facing the wind she untied her ponytail and let her long dark hair stream out behind her.

She turned to Rick. "So, tell me: where did you go?"

"I had my bike. I bought a tent and made for the Isle of Skye. The rain and the wind suited my mood. I went for walks in the shadow of the Black Cuillin, just calling her name. I could not stop crying."

"You're hurting but you're strong. You'll be alright. We're together now."

Rick put out a hand to touch her. She felt real enough; taking his hand in both of hers she pulled him to her and held on, while he sobbed.

"Never let me go."

THE END

Road trip Isfahan 1969

Acknowledgment.

I am grateful to all the lovely people who inspired and made this novel possible, for their help, criticism and support. You know who you are so I feel no need to add a long list of names.

Road trip Isfahan 1969

Notes on the Text

1. The government was trying to stem the flow of money out of the country by restricting the number of travellers' cheques each person could take on holiday to £50, equivalent to £700 in 2015. There were twenty shilling in the pound and twelve pence in a shilling.

2. 100 Persian rials = 10/- = 50p or £7 in 2015.

3. BUNAC: British Universities North America Club

The Land Rover gave no trouble. It covered 10,000 miles over 40 days driving and used about 400 gallons (2,000 litres) of petrol, two pints (one litre) of oil and hardly any water, at the cost of about £100, equivalent to £1400 in 2015.

Printed in Great Britain
by Amazon